When Your Heart Starts to Cry

BY KAYE KARR

DORRANCE
PUBLISHING CO
EST. 1920
PITTSBURGH, PENNSYLVANIA 15238

Dorrance Publishing Co
585 Alpha Drive
Pittsburgh, PA 15238
Visit our website at *www.dorrancebookstore.com*

ISBN: 978-1-6470-2356-0
eISBN: 978-1-6470-2810-7

Acknowledgments

This book is dedicated to my father, Eugene Wm. Grantham. My thanks to him for spending hours and hours telling and retelling me stories of his youth. And to my brother, Lonnie Grantham, who served in the US Navy stationed on the Azores Islands. Also, I want to acknowledge Keith Grantham. I am very proud to call him my "little" brother.

A million thanks to my husband, Fred. He is my encourager, my critic, my proofreader, and my love.

I am so grateful to my family. They are my cheerleaders.
Todd and Joanne Starnes (Emily, Nathan, Cole)
Cory and Catherine Starnes (Elizabeth and Jennifer)
Janene Grantham Staley

Contents

Chapter 1 - circa 1945

LOVE ONCE REMOVED

Labor had been normal - excruciating pain, screaming, crying and praying that it would be over soon.

Joseph Eugene Hoffman was born in a Detroit Hospital.

The child was a healthy boy with a full head of dark hair. He was a nice-looking baby with a bit of reddish tint to his wrinkled little body. He wasn't round nor was he chubby. He weighed in at almost seven pounds. Joseph wasn't squirming and wriggling like Georgina's first son, Harold, who was at home with his father. Only God knew what was taking place there as dear ol' daddy, Carl, liked to have a few highballs about this time of day and drink until he fell onto his bed in a stupor.

At least Georgina knew what to expect this time in the delivery room. She was thinking about her own mother who, when she was pregnant with Georgina, didn't have any idea how the baby would get out of her tummy. She thought that somehow her belly button would open up and expand enough for the doctor to reach in and pull the infant out. Those were the dark ages when ladies didn't talk about men, sex, babies, bodies or birth.

This second child she would name Joseph. He had a pleasant, almost peaceful aura about him. Sadly, when the nurse put him to Georgina's breast, Georgina barely looked down at him. She let the little bundle search with its tiny lips instinctively open in a hunt for her nipple. She wasn't about to help in this disgusting ritual. Sucking on her breasts for sustenance repulsed her.

1

She had bottles at home that had been used by Harold, and she couldn't wait to prop one of those bottles up against a pillow and stick it in this slurping little mouth. If he were to move too much and the bottle's nipple fell out of his mouth, oh well, that was not her problem. Her job was to provide some sort of nourishment. If he didn't drink what she provided, *it wasn't her fault.*

Baby Joseph's home was in a quaint little brick bungalow on a very typical tree-lined street in Detroit. His three-year-old brother, Harold, wasn't happy about sharing his room with a baby and wasn't happy about sharing what little adult attention he was getting with this new little intruder.

Georgina was not, to put it mildly, "the motherly type." She often stuffed down the feelings of resentment she had toward both of her two unsuspecting and neglected sons. She began to feel as though they were holding her hostage and forcing her into a life of service to them. Somehow, Harold didn't irritate her the way the little one did. At least Harold could walk and she didn't have to touch him very often. She only had to help him dress and to give him an occasional bath. Now if they were out in public, which was seldom, she would have to wipe his nose for him or what would people think?

On the other hand there was Joseph. The little one cried when he was wet; he cried when he was hungry, and he just cried whenever he felt like it. Cry, cry, cry. Georgina did not have the affection for him that was needed to meet such responsibility. She walked the floor, she bit her nails, she stared out the window not really looking at anything, just staring into space for long periods of time. She emotionally removed herself. She shut out everyone, and to her husband, Carl, she was frigid. He found his feeling of well-being in a bottle of liquor. For him, whiskey was always comforting, soothing and numbing.

Too much alcohol, too many mouths to feed, too many bills, and facing life with a heartless wife, a loveless marriage and unending years of responsibility ahead of him, Carl escaped. In the haze of a hangover, he left his wife and two little sons for the bright lights of New York City. He felt there had to be something better for him and in a place as big as New York, there had to be new possibilities. Without a word to Georgina or a pat on the heads of his little boys, he took their only car and drove away with one suitcase which held a few clothes including his one suit. He did not bother to even take a photograph or two with him, and he didn't make an effort to glance back over his shoulder. He just pushed down hard on the accelerator and sped off. He truly never cared if he ever saw Georgina, Harold, or Joseph again.

Georgina pretended to sleep and acted as if she didn't hear her husband fumbling around and fighting with that old suitcase in the back of their closet. She had a feeling of relief when she saw, out of her almost opened eye, that he was going out the door with suitcase in hand. Now if she could get rid of more of her burdens, she could to start to live again. Little Joseph had to go!

Georgina's mother had left her an inheritance that she never got around to telling Carl about. Well, he would have spent it at the local beer garden. He didn't know that Georgina could pay the hospital bills and the rent with enough left over to sustain the little family. Georgina would just hire a babysitter and return to her job at Hudson's Department Store. Someone else could take care of those two boys.

Georgina's workmate was Margaret Graham, "Maggie" to most people. In contrast, Maggie was married but had no children. It's not as if she didn't try. She could not conceive a child even though she tried and tried with every Tom, Dick, or Harry. Her husband, Stan, closed a blind eye to her frequent indiscretions. Incredibly, he loved her. She was tall, slim, with chestnut-colored hair and hazel-colored eyes. She was nice to look at, and she carried herself like a lioness in heat. Many were her lovers but no one man for long. She liked the newness of each conquest. Every affair came with a new bedroom technique, a new man, a new way, and a new style. She loved it all. If her latest paramour had a little money to spend, he was on her mind and there would definitely be more than one tryst. Maggie's job at Hudson's in downtown Detroit was only a short bus ride from her apartment. Hudson's was the department store of choice for the upscale shoppers in those days. Work gave her plenty of opportunities to meet men in the way of customers. She could easily snare a guy if she liked the way he wore his hair, or the way he walked, or if she liked the way he dressed, or if he just looked like he could be looking for a good time. She appeared to be reserved and professional. On the contrary, under that facade was a grossly vulgar woman who was mysteriously attractive in her improper lifestyle. Maggie considered Georgina her friend. They had met at Hudson's a few years ago. She knew that Georgina was married and had a couple kids. She also knew that Georgina was not taking well to motherhood. The two often talked over lunch in the breakroom where their lockers stored their handbags, coats, umbrellas, boots, and some sort of a light lunch or a snack that they had brought from home. There was no refrigerator available to them. Food brought from home was always nonperishable. Just a piece of fruit, maybe an apple and a few crackers with a cup of tea were the fare. Both women were in their early twenties and restless.

Maggie was curious because Georgina rarely spoke of her two sons. Georgina wasn't one to talk about her personal life. She was quiet and mostly kept to herself. She was friendly enough but somewhat detached. Always helpful to customers but no one got through that wall she had up around herself and soon no one cared enough to try. At home, she barely tended to her two boys who desperately ached for her to just glance their way for a moment. They longed for the closeness of a hug or even just a smile from their mother. She chose to ignore them.

Georgina spent her time in private thoughts, spiraling down, feeling sorry for herself. She felt like an animal that had one foot snared in a trap and couldn't get away unless she chewed off her own snared foot.

Meanwhile, Maggie vacillated between what it might be like to be a mother and/or keeping the freedom to focus on herself and her own selfish needs. In reality, she no longer had that choice due to a decision she made when she was barely a teenager. She found herself remembering that tall, lanky boy in her English class who walked her home from school almost every afternoon. He was handsome and she liked him. Spring was in the air, birds were singing and the breeze was blowing soft and warm. As they reached her house, she didn't say "*no*" when he asked if he could come in.

No one was home, and the temptation of lying together on her bed was enticing to each of them. He was eager to take Maggie's hand and pull her onto her own bed. Maggie's mother was at the church setting up for the bazaar. Maggie had the house all to herself for a few hours.

Her childhood bed was lined with stuffed animals - a bear, an elephant, a giraffe, and even a green turtle. They all seemed to be watching, but that didn't stop the two teenagers from stretching out on the pink chenille bedspread that covered her little twin-sized bed. He gave Maggie a look that was of such hunger and desire for her that she felt new sensations and a longing she had never known before. Somehow, she knew instinctively, by nature, this was how women must feel when they experience passion.

Maggie seemed to melt when he kissed her. She kissed him back with an ardor that she didn't know existed deep within her being. She pressed even closer to him with sensuous desire. The teenagers hadn't intended to lose control and go all the way but for the first time for both of them they submitted to their bodies and had intercourse. She, being a virgin, felt the slight sting and tear of her hymen being ripped causing a slight bit of blood, but she could not stop moving with the rhythm of his body on top of her.

When it was over, they were embarrassed, scared, and shy with one another and nervous about the possibility of her mother walking in on them. Neither of them ever planned to take such a chance.

They avoided each other at school the next day and the next day and the next. The young couple never spoke another word to each other. He didn't walk with her anymore. He began taking the long way home six blocks out of his way so he wouldn't have to go by her house. His father was being transferred to Atlanta sometime in the next few months. He had been angry about leaving and starting a new school, but now the move couldn't come soon enough for him.

When Maggie didn't get her period that month, she barely gave it a serious thought. The possibility of being pregnant and having a child growing inside her had never entered her mind. Not long after the missed monthly bleeding, Maggie's mother heard her being sick in the middle of the night. She awoke to the sounds of her daughter throwing up the meatloaf they had eaten for dinner. She waited until the heaving subsided and ventured in to see what was going on. Maggie was as surprised as anyone. She was not prone to stomach problems. There must be a flu bug going around.

When Maggie got up the next morning, she looked pale. She felt exhausted, and there was no sparkle in her pretty hazel-colored eyes. She liked school and wanted to go today because they were having a special speaker coming to talk about leprosy in third-world countries. He was bringing pictures of the poor, unfortunate victims of the disease. Rumor had it that some of the pictures were of people who only had stumps where fingers and toes used to be.

She didn't want to miss the gore of it all, but she felt lightheaded and out of sorts. There *must* be something going around. She got herself together enough to walk the four blocks to school and slipped into her desk chair. She didn't talk to her friends because she felt so queasy that she didn't want to waste energy saying good morning to the bright shiny faces around her.

The speaker began his presentation about people who are sick and maimed. They were referred to as lepers. He passed around grayish, faded photos that were very worn from the many hands that had previously held them. As the first picture came into Maggie's view, she glanced at it and then quickly found the classroom door and stumbled out into the hallway. Down the hall she found the door that said "GIRLS" and shoved it open. Once inside she fell to her knees on the cold, tile floor in front of the porcelain toilet bowl just in time to heave her insides into it.

When she opened her eyes, she saw that the toilet had not been flushed by the previous user and that a brown turd was floating amid her vomit. At that point, she literally wretched from deep, deep within her being.

The school secretary, Mrs. Lorenz, was in somewhat of a rush to use the restroom and get back to her desk. She wore her reading glasses around her neck dangling from a beaded cord. Her gray hair was always in a tight bun on top of her head and her hand habitually went to the nape of her neck checking to make sure that no straggling hairs had come loose. Maggie heard the quick steps, the click, click, click of Mrs. Lorenz's high heels pass her stall and enter into the stall next to hers. It only took a second for Mrs. Lorenz to realize something was wrong next door. She could smell toilet smells and puke. She relieved herself before she called out, "Who is in here?"

There was silence. Again, she asked and her question was met again with silence. She, being a prim and proper employee of the school system, was very aware that she may be invading someone's privacy, but she quietly bent down to peek under the metal door to see what might be going on and maybe identify the gross smell coming from the third stall. Mrs. Lorenz could never have guessed what she would discover behind that locked door. It was Margaret Graham curled up on the floor. Margaret was not moving.

Mrs. Lorenz called out to her, "Margaret, Margaret Graham is that you? Are you all right, dear?" There was no answer.

That might have been a foolish question after seeing Margaret all crumpled up on the bathroom floor and obviously *not all right*, but she didn't know what else to say. She tried to open the door, which was against every bit of her rigid upbringing. It just wouldn't open. Mrs. Lorenz reached under the door and kind of poked at Margaret. Then she lightly tapped on Margaret's right leg and then slightly wiggled her left foot. Nothing. No movement, no sound.

She said, "Don't worry Margaret. I'll be right back. I'm going to get your teacher."

As Mrs. Lorenz stepped into the hallway, she heard the principal, Mr. Collins, excusing students for lunch break - which also meant bathroom break.

Mrs. Lorenz immediately knew she had to stop students from coming into the girls' bathroom to use the toilets and wash up before eating lunch. She immediately went into combat mode; she had to stop anyone from coming into the restroom. She closed the bathroom door, went into the hall, and stood guard in front of it.

She put on her professional office secretary face and spoke in her authoritative, practiced voice quietly announcing to each girl who came towards her that the restroom was closed due to a plumbing problem. The girls were routed to the only other 'ladies' room down on the first floor next to the gymnasium. There was some grumbling, but for the most part the students were so happy to be out of the classroom and away from the pictures of lepers that they filed on down the stairs without too much commotion.

Mrs. Lorenz heard her office phone ringing faintly in the distance. She had been faithful to always answering every call by the second ring no matter what, but now, she would not leave her post in front of the bathroom door.

She was hoping that Miss Smith, Maggie's teacher, would need to use the commode and leave her classroom for a moment or two.

Mr. Collins, the high school principal, looked down the hall at his dutiful secretary and wondered what had come over her. *Mrs. Lorenz was standing in front of the girls' bathroom and for Pete's sake why wasn't she in the office answering her ringing phone?* As he approached her, she waved him away. She couldn't possibly talk to Mr. Collins about bathroom situations. She mouthed to him to please get Miss Smith.

As he came closer and she whispered, "Get Miss Smith. It's ...um...um... kind of an emergency."

Mr. Collins had never seen Mrs. Lorenz with even a hair out of place, let alone lose any of her stoic composure; and he had never known her to not pick up the phone whenever it rang. Now here she was mouthing something to him and even though she still had not totally dropped her demeanor of perfection, he was getting some weird vibrations from his trustworthy office assistant. It was somewhat unsettling to him.

As he walked nearer to her, she waved him away and said out loud, "Miss Smith." Although he was not privy to Mrs. Lorenz's classified information, he obediently turned and took some quick, long strides towards Classroom 212 and Miss Smith. He liked Miss Smith. She was kind and seemed to have honest concern for the wellbeing of her students. She was blonde and blue eyed and even though he tried not to notice, she was very pretty. She was twenty-nine and walked with a slightly crooked gait.

Mr. Collins didn't know her well enough to know that her leg injury had been caused by a motorcycle accident. She had been riding with her brother on a highway in Saginaw, Michigan. Miss Smith always hated motorbikes. Her friend in college had been paralyzed from the waist down in a motorbike accident during their sophomore year.

Miss Smith's accident happened one afternoon when she was tucked in tightly behind her big brother zooming down a highway that was still under construction. The highway wasn't open to traffic yet, so Miss Smith and her brother were the only ones touring that stretch. Unbeknown to either of them, this unfinished highway ended in a ten-foot drop-off similar to the brink of a pier. This road was closed because it temporarily ended in midair. When her brother concluded that they were soon going to be air-borne, he hollered for her to hang on. She did. They flew into the air and came bouncing down onto gravel where the bike slid on its side before finally coming to a stop. They might have been killed as the road construction workers could do nothing except stand there watching. Some of the workmen just shook their heads and called Miss Smith and her brother stupid, dumb sons of bitches, all the while leaning against their shovels and spitting on the ground. It was hard to believe that the only injury was Miss Smith's fractured right ankle, which never recovered completely.

Mr. Collins was taking pleasure thinking about Miss Smith, when he came to his senses and remembered that Mrs. Lorenz was standing guard outside the girls' lavatory. He peered through the transom in the door of Miss Smith's room. He was 6'1" and even he had to stretch his neck to see into her room. The window was small and placed almost at the top of her door. He saw she was washing the blackboard with a damp rag. He smiled when he noticed a small bright red apple on the corner of her desk. He guessed an admiring student had shyly given it to her that morning in an attempt to show her his thoughtfulness. Mr. Collins wouldn't have blamed him for trying to get her attention with a gift. Now his thoughts were becoming a little improper as a high school principal. Immediately, he snapped himself out of his daydream and tapped lightly on the classroom door before opening it.

It would not have been respectful to just open it and walk in unexpectedly. She turned to face him as he was trying not to take pleasure in looking at her and being alone with her. Yes, he remembered that he was a married man and he knew that he would never say or do anything that could be misconstrued as inappropriate.

Miss Smith put down the cleaning rag and wiped her hands on a square of cotton toweling. The look on her face was soft but inquiring. He cleared his throat and told her of Mrs. Lorenz standing in front of the girls' bathroom and asking him to fetch her. This was so out of the ordinary that Miss Smith quickly rushed past Mr. Collins and was out the door and down the hall before he could compose himself. Miss Smith saw Mrs. Lorenz placed solidly in front of the door. The boys' football team couldn't have shoved her out of the way as she was determined not to let anyone by her.

"What's wrong, Mrs. Lorenz?" Miss Smith asked as she cocked her head to the side as if to hear better.

Mrs. Lorenz cupped her mouth with her hands and whispered into Miss Smith's ear that Margaret Graham was lying on the floor and wasn't moving. Miss Smith stepped around her and acted. She called out, "Maggie, what's wrong? Please let me help you." There was no answer only a soft moan came from the stall.

"If you don't talk to me, Maggie, I'm going to crawl under this door. Do you hear me? I'm coming in there."

Again, a slight moan was the only sound. Nothing was working. Miss Smith had to do something. She got on her hands and knees and squeezed herself under the door of the stall. She straddled Maggie's feet and reached up to unlock the door. She needed to create more room and get some air to defuse the horrible stench coming from the toilet. She was able to lean over just far enough to push the handle down and flush the commode. Miss Smith grabbed a handful of toilet paper, wadded it up while getting to the sink to run water on it. She sat down on the floor and bathed Maggie. First her eyes and then her face as she tried to revive her with the wet tissue. She reached up to flush the toilet again thinking there was still waste left in it just as Maggie opened her eyes slightly. They both wanted to cry but Maggie was much too weak to cry and Miss Smith needed to remain strong for her anguishing student.

Mrs. Lorenz had entered the room on tiptoe and was now standing a few feet away from the two who were wrapped in each other's arms while sitting on the cold floor. She was just quietly staring down at them hoping someone would say something. Finally, Miss Smith looked up and asked, "Will you phone Maggie's mother? Maggie is in need of medical attention." While they waited, the bathroom remained off limits to everyone.

Velma Graham arrived. She had received the call from Mrs. Lorenz and had walked the four blocks to school wearing her best coat and hat because the phone call seemed very important. She went right to the office where Mrs. Lorenz was waiting to escort her to the girls' bathroom. Velma knew Maggie was feeling a little under the weather and she vaguely remembered hearing her being sick during the night.

Maggie's mother was not prepared for what she saw huddled in the bathroom stall. She bent over and pulled Maggie to her feet. She struggled to support most of her daughter's weight with her arms wrapped around her waist. Maggie's almost limp body was against her mother's hip. This may have looked like a normal thing for a mother to do for her daughter but Velma was rarely this close to Maggie. She seldom hugged her because that was the way *she* was raised and now family touching was uncomfortable. She managed a fake smile to Miss Smith and then to Mrs. Lorenz and began the four blocks walk home. She took small baby steps all the way while holding up Maggie who wasn't protesting.

When they were in the privacy of their house, Velma asked, "Maggie, what happened at school this morning?"

Maggie told her mother the truth, "I don't know what happened to me." She weakly turned and disappeared into her room where her warm bed was waiting to comfort her.

Doctor visits were not routine and only made when all other options failed. Velma made an appointment with Dr. Williams, the only doctor they knew. He was a family physician, and his office wasn't very far away.

Living in Detroit there was no reason to own a car as there were buses, taxis, and feet to get you wherever you had to go. Velma walked or took the bus most of the time. For *this* doctor visit she made an exception. She splurged and called a cab.

Fear was seeping into her thoughts about Maggie.

Chapter 2

LOVE KILLED

*D*r. Williams was middle-aged, married and had a family. In fact, he had three daughters of his own. He entered the examining room with an air of confidence and a stethoscope curved around his neck. He instinctively evaluated this sickly little sixteen-year-old. Then he politely asked Velma to leave for the moment and relax in the waiting room.

He had his nurse, Carolyn, attend to Maggie with him. He never examined a female patient without the protection of one of his nurses in case there were ever a question of impropriety. After closing the door for privacy, he looked closely into Maggie's lifeless eyes. Learning of her queasiness, Dr. Williams cautiously asked, "Maggie, could there be a chance that you are pregnant?" Maggie was completely dumbfounded that he would ask such a question.

"Of course not!" she answered, confused and offended by him asking such an outrageous thing. When he asked her if she had ever had sexual relations, she blushed and told him, "No." That's when it hit her like a sucker punch. An afternoon encounter in her bedroom with that guy from her English class. The boy who used to walk her home after school. It couldn't be conceivable. A few minutes of sex with someone couldn't mean she was pregnant. She looked at the floor of the examining room and vomited again, splashing a few driblets of yellowish bile on Carolyn's white nurse's shoes.

Dr. Williams was intuitive, wise and suspicious. He took blood and urine samples and sent her home with orders of complete bed rest until the test results came back. She was not to go to school until he gave her a release.

Maggie spent most of the next two days in her room, not eating much because she couldn't keep much down. Occasionally she sipped on tea and ate tiny bites of toast with a little grape jam. She wasn't feeling much better the next week when she and her mother went to see Dr. Williams for her scheduled follow-up appointment. Nurse Carolyn opened the waiting room door and escorted Maggie down the hall and into Room 2.

Velma hurried to use the bathroom and returned to realize that she wasn't being included in the doctor's consultation. Carolyn told Maggie that she did not have to disrobe and that Dr. Williams would be in shortly. Maggie was feeling weak. She was pale and disturbingly thin.

When Dr. Williams entered the small sterile room, Maggie was sitting with her head down and did not look up at him. He crossed the room and gently took her hand in his left and with his right hand he tenderly coaxed her chin up so that their eyes met. He was a kind man and came from a family of seven brothers and sisters. He had put himself through the University of Michigan Medical School and loved his profession most days. This wasn't one of those days.

He looked into Maggie's sunken dark-rimmed eyes which were filling up with tears. She looked back into his all-knowing doctor eyes as he told her that he had the results of her tests. She continued to stare at him while trying to brace herself for what he might tell her.

His voice was firm and assuring when he said, "You are going to be just fine. The outcomes of the tests we ran indicated that you do not have an illness."

She started to breathe a bit easier and relaxed her shoulders somewhat.

He continued, "You are, however, going to need further medical care." She did not utter a word trying hard to process what he was saying. "Maggie," he said gently but with authority while still holding her hand, "your pregnancy tests were positive."

She felt like she would faint. This couldn't be happening. She started to shake and then she started to sob. She thought she was going to vomit, yet all she produced were dry heaves - gagging over and over. "Can you tell me who the father is?" he asked. She didn't answer.

Dr. Williams addressed Carolyn, "Please ask Mrs. Graham to join us."
Then to Maggie, as he adjusted his glasses, he asked, "Do you want to tell your
mother yourself or do you prefer that I tell her?"

Maggie shuddered, "What? Why do we have to tell her?"

"You are a minor and she is responsible for you. I'll tell her," he said.

Velma was taken aback when she saw the condition of her only child who
was shaking, breathing heavily and trying to stuff down sobs. Maggie looked
so forlorn and so small and so young. She wondered if Maggie were going to
die right then and there. Velma mentally braced herself for what Dr. Williams
was telling her. ***What? No - Maggie - pregnant?*** Velma slowly sat down onto
the hard, straight back chair that was closest to her. She felt humiliated and
wished at that moment Maggie really would die.

Dr. Williams was going on about options that were available to unwed
mothers. He suggested a loving comfortable cottage environment that was
sponsored by the Sisters of Grace in Wisconsin. He said, "I can use a little of
my influence to secure a place for Maggie. The facility was one of the best in
the nation at placing babies in loving homes. I assure you that no one need
know. I'm sorry Maggie, but you should make your decision in the next month
before you start to 'show'."

Dr. Williams and his staff would help in any way they could. It was Maggie's decision to make whether to keep her child or let the little one be adopted
out to a good family. No one else would ever have to be told. Everything would
be kept very confidential. A story could be made up that Maggie was doing an
exchange student program and was studying abroad for a year. Velma just sat
there staring at Dr. Williams. She was speechless. There had to be some mistake she thought. Margaret Graham could not be pregnant. . . *She was not that
kind of girl. . . He must be wrong. . . It could not be true!*

The ride going home in the cab was quiet except for the occasional squawk
from the driver's radio. Neither mother nor daughter could look at the other.
In a thirty-minute conversation, Dr. Williams had turned their world upside
down. How dare he say such things? When they reached their house, Maggie
went straight to her room and laid herself down on the pink chenille bedspread
in the very place where her life as she knew it came to an end. Velma put down
her purse and silently made a cup of tea, she didn't know what else to do. She
had to have time to think. She absolutely could not become a grandmother while
her only child was an unmarried teenager. She had to consider the options.

Maggie stayed in her room until the next morning. She had come out just once earlier to use the bathroom. Her mother had slept only a few hours. She had been concocting a plan of her own to save her daughter and herself. She would stop all this insanity of a pregnant sixteen-year-old daughter. When the two of them met in the kitchen, Velma gave Maggie a glance and told her not to worry and that she would help her get rid of this dirty little problem. She didn't ask who the father was. She didn't want to know.

Spring break was only a few days away, meaning there would be no school for ten days counting weekends. She would have to hurry with her plan. She went to the medicine cabinet in the bathroom and found her stash of anti-depressants. She then went to the hall closet and picked out a coat hanger. She found one that was fairly flexible. Maggie had sipped a small glass of water and was in bed lying curled up in a fetal position with her eyes tightly closed. Velma shook her a little and said, "Wake up and look at me; I'm going to help you by doing a little cleaning of your female area." Maggie was too tired, distracted and weak to care about anything her mother was saying.

Velma gave her daughter a nice cool drink of lemonade which she had prepared especially for her. Maggie made a face when she tasted it but her mother told her to drink it down or she would pour it down her throat herself. After the lemonade was gone, Velma left the room to let the drink take effect. She had laced the lemonade with some of her own sedatives and a few ounces of vodka. Her lovely, unsuspecting daughter would soon be out like a light.

Velma reentered the room to find Maggie very groggy and lethargic. She shook Maggie a little and ordered her to take off her underpants. Maggie was in a deep, dreamlike state. She obeyed her mother, and with a little help, she was naked from the waist down. Velma hurried to get the coat hanger. She untwisted it so that it became one long wire with a hook on one end. She squeezed the hook to make it narrow enough to insert into her daughter. She called out to Maggie to see if she were awake. There was no response. That lemonade cocktail seemed to have done the trick. Maggie was nearly unconscious.

Velma rolled Maggie onto her back and forced her knees up and forced her thighs apart. She took the wire coat hanger and held it in her hand. She called out loudly this time to Maggie, still again there was no response. Maggie had fallen into a deep, deep sleep. Good! Velma inserted the narrow hook inside her daughter. She eased the wire in a little farther, and a little farther, so she could scrape and dislodge anything growing inside Maggie. Her sleeping daughter's face tightened and she started to squirm a little. Velma told her to be still and that she was almost finished. Maggie screamed but did not become fully awake.

Velma was satisfied that nothing could live after her procedure was finished and blood was running freely onto the towels she had placed under Maggie's hips. Maggie was groaning and whimpering but still did not wake up completely. Velma gently removed the wire hanger and got rid of it by hiding it behind an old cabinet in the cellar. She then made a cup of tea and drank it from her favorite china teacup while sitting on the side of Maggie's little twin-sized bed waiting for her to wake.

She did wake. Yes, indeed she did. She was wracked with pain and bleeding heavily. She stared at her mother with fearful, questioning eyes. Her mother said, "You will have to endure this pain but now you are free from a future of being an unwed-teenaged mother of a little bastard. If all goes as planned, you can go back to school after spring break with everyone else." Maggie was disturbingly depressed. She was pale and thin, nevertheless, no one would ever have to know why.

Miss Smith, Mrs. Lorenz and Mr. Collins all knew that Maggie had been sick. They would be told that she had suffered a bad case of influenza. Velma would contact Dr. Williams and tell him that Maggie had a miscarriage and his services would no longer be needed.

That lie had worked very well for the next five years until Maggie decided to marry a decent man who was considered a good catch in his day. His name was Stanley but his friends called him Stan.

Chapter 3

LOVE MISLED

S tan first saw Maggie at the soda fountain in Donaldson's Drug Store on the corner of Washington and Main. She didn't stand out from the other girls in looks, even so, there was something about her that captured his attention. It was her sexiness. The way she looked at him while she crossed her legs in a not so ladylike way revealing a little more than what was appropriate.

It didn't matter that Stan was older than Maggie by almost fifteen years; he was smitten by her. Maggie never knew her dad. She never knew the love of a father. She was told that he had been killed in a tree trimming accident when she was an infant. Unconsciously, she was drawn to father figures. She had always been attracted to older men. She was also looking for a way to get out from under her mother's control. Consequently, after only a few dates, Stan and Maggie planned an outdoor casual wedding to be held at a small, inexpensive resort in Canada.

It was mid-July and the temperature was registering in the 90s with humidity to match. It had rained for most of the week before the wedding and had rained the morning of the celebration. The ground was soggy. The tables and chairs were set up under a canvas canopy where it was at least 100 degrees. The mosquitoes were swarming in thick clouds everywhere. The folding chairs looked very nice with white ribbons tied around the backs. The tables were covered with white cotton table clothes that were meant to look like linen. The centerpieces were beautiful roses that had been grown in the hothouse behind the old inn where the wedding party and guests were staying. The view from the inn was very nice with the lake and beach complete with sailboats, swimmers and sunbathers. The inn had been rather elegant in its day. As time passed, the hotel had become old and outdated. Nowadays, it was considered quaint with charm and character. The rooms and services had become affordable.

The day of the wedding was hot and very wet. The guests were starting to gather and as they sat on the folding chairs placed around the oblong tables, the weight of the guests caused the chairs to start sinking into the soft, soggy ground. The heavier the guest, the deeper the chair sank until some of their chins were nearly resting on the table in front of them. The hotter it got, the more wine they drank and the more they sank. No one wanted to be cast as a complainer so when they saw the best man, who weighed in at nearly 270 pounds, just barely peeking over the edge of the table because his chair was halfway into the boggy wet ground, they just laughed and slapped another mosquito.

Time was passing slowly and to add to the misery, the wedding was detained by about twenty minutes because the maid-of-honor was locked inside her room at the inn. The locks were ancient and it was so humid that her room's lock was hopelessly stuck. It took her twenty minutes to pull, tug and saw with a nail file to free herself from captivity. When she finally arrived at the tent, she was upset and embarrassed about being late and holding up the proceedings. She was sopping wet from perspiration and her hair was hanging in her eyes. What curl was meant to be there wasn't anywhere to be found. Her makeup had run in all the wrong directions and her lavender organza 'maid of honor' dress was no longer crisp. There were telltale signs of earlier tears of frustration. The once beautiful dress hung nearly to her ankles like a wet dishrag.

When the ceremony started, the minister stood under the canopy with his back to the inn. To receive their vows, the bridal couple stood facing him. The bridal party of six made a half circle behind the bride and groom while the guests all gathered behind them. Everyone was facing the inn except the minister as he began with a prayer. The guests were having a difficult time focusing on the nuptials because of the merciless heat, humidity, high heels stuck in the mud and bugs.

As if that weren't bad enough, just to the right of the tent a middle-aged woman in a skimpy bathing suit, who had been sunbathing on the beach, was attempting to get to her room at the inn. Almost all of the wedding guests could see her easily and like a train wreck, it was hard not to look. She was way too out of shape to wear such a revealing swim suit as she was kind of stuffed into it. To combat the heat, she had been drinking gin and tonic on the rocks since breakfast.

She was tipsy and struggling to get up a small hill. When she noticed the wedding taking place, she reached into her beach bag fumbling for her camera. She finally found it and was trying to get a good picture of the wedding party as she took a step back to face the group. Being a little intoxicated, barefooted and with the sun in her eyes, she lost her balance and fell backwards into the bushes that surrounded the inn.

Most of the wedding guests witnessed the lady's butt backing into the shrubs and in a matter of seconds all they could see of her were her feet sticking straight up kicking in the air with no signs of the rest of her. She was thrashing around and swearing under her breath.

Out of respect for the bride and groom, no one went to rescue the lady in the bushes. They didn't want to interrupt the ceremony. They could see the bushes moving and the lady crawling out. She was disoriented and had scratches all over her much too-exposed body. No one wanted to take attention away from the reason they were there. However, it was hard not to offer some help and even harder not to laugh as she stumbled from out of the shrubs dragging a towel that was covered with little twigs, all the while hanging onto her beach bag that was leaking suntan oil.

Everyone's attention soon returned to the ceremony as Maggie and Stan were pronounced husband and wife. The couple opened up the celebration by dancing. The big band sound was the music of the era and almost everyone got up to dance in the soggy grass. It seemed as though a new dance craze was being born with rhythmic moves on the mucky ground (squish, squish) while slapping at the zillion mosquitoes that were biting any exposed skin (slap, slap). It was a new and different way of dancing to say the least.

The band members had quite a challenge when it came to playing their instruments and singing while battling the relentless buzzing bugs. As the lead singer was holding a long high note, a moth fluttered into his mouth and got caught behind his front teeth. He went on singing while swallowing the moth alive. He never missed a note and the beat went on. Most people have had butterflies in their stomachs but moths – probably not. In spite of all of that, Maggie and Stan were now married.

Stan so wanted to start a family. After two years of trying to conceive, Maggie made an appointment with a gynecologist. The examination confirmed what she suspected. Her female organs had been so badly damaged years ago by her mother, that she would certainly not know pregnancy. It all came flooding back to her memory. *The day her mother had injured her and had left her ruined.* She and her mother never mentioned that day, not even to each other. Maggie had gone back to school and graduated with her class the following year.

Maggie used an appointment with the gynecologist to deceive Stan. She lied to him and said, "The specialist told me that I am a healthy young woman and that it must be my husband's fault that there are no children." Then she added, "You're probably sterile."

Hearing this heartbreaking news, Stan bowed his head and put his hands over his face. He was so ashamed. He felt that he was less of a man and that he had let his wife down. He begged her to forgive him and apologized to her for his inadequacy. Stan was hanging his head unable to look at her, when he whispered, "I'm so sorry."

They were never to be parents, and Maggie made him think it was all because of him. He secretly grieved the rest of his life, never knowing that it was not true. It had been a lie.

As a result, when Maggie started having sexual partners behind his back, he pretended not to notice. He felt she must need other men since he had failed her so profoundly.

Stan knew Maggie had always been a flirt and that she had been unfaithful.

She had mastered when, at a crucial moment, to lift her skirt slightly to give a private showing while adjusting her garter. Stan wasn't aware of the times she said she was meeting Georgina after work for a bite to eat, when actually she was filled with excitement and arousal because instead of meeting her lady friend, she was really all sweaty and hot thinking about her latest sexual fantasy with her newest conquest.

Maggie would wonder what this new guy would talk about. He had better *not* talk about a wife or a kid. If he had to talk at all, she wanted it to be about her. How good she looked, how her body was his dream come true or how her dark brown tresses were like silk to his touch. No questions please! Questions were off limits. Not "Are you married?" "Where do you live?" Who cared? Maggie's goal for the two of them was to enjoy each other and not to think or to talk of anything else. She always hoped her newest guy would not fall asleep after their fun was over. She hated a sleeping man. She no longer found anything attractive about her lover if he fell asleep. He might even snore or drool. *YUCK!* Her only thought was, "*Get me out of here. I need to get to the downtown bus depot by 7:00 PM.*" If her lover fell asleep, then he was no longer paying attention to her, now was he? She would often moan loudly in his ear in an attempt to wake him. If that didn't work, she would fake a cough or a loud sneeze. Sometimes she would purposely trip over a shoe and clumsily stumble across the room. Maybe even falling so her knight in shining armor could sweep her up for another round of heavy breathing. When she was done in the bedroom, she was done with the relationship. "Just wake up, jerk, and get out. *Get your rumpled clothes, find your socks and say your goodbyes.*" Her lovers were never as appealing when they were leaving the love nest as when they were entering her wanting presence.

Maggie was getting to know that little shy lady, Georgina, whom she worked with at Hudson's. She knew Georgina had two very young sons and she also knew of her struggles with working and raising little kids.

Georgina shared with Maggie some of her frustrations and once she said she wished she could give her children away. "*I should just give them to you and your husband,*" she said and gave an embarrassed little laugh after suggesting such an idea – truthfully, she had been thinking about that very thing.

A few days later while having tea during their work break, Maggie abruptly said, "Okay, I've talked it over with my husband. We'll take the little one."

Georgina looked at her in disbelief.

Maggie continued, "If you meant it about giving us your boys, we'll take the little one. The little one because he is still too young to remember you. We would want to raise him as our own. Stan wants a son much more than I do. He thinks he is sterile and longs to be a dad. He says he will take most of the responsibility for the baby's care. He wants to adopt him and give him his surname. Stan would have an heir. We would insist on never telling him you birthed him. If you decide that you want to see him from time to time, we will tell him that you are his *aunt* and that his older brother is his *cousin*." Maggie stopped talking and took a sip of her tea that was getting cold.

Georgina gasped and looked at the door making sure that it was closed and no one could hear her when she agreed to Maggie's demands.

Georgina looked across the table at Maggie and was nearly whispering when she told her, "I know I'm not a good mother. I don't like kids. I like being here at work. I love the beautiful china and flatware that I sell. I don't like going home and being a mommy. I might like to see him on occasion, although I will agree to your terms."

Georgina choked a little then swallowed. She could manage her older son and soon she wouldn't have to put up with the baby. She gave an almost audible cry of relief and gratefulness.

Void of any further emotion Georgina said, "The little one's name is Joseph Eugene."

Chapter 4

LOVE FOUND

*S*tan and Maggie went to Georgina's house that weekend to pick up little Joseph.

As soon as Stan saw the boy, he got down on his knees and looked into the toddler's beautiful blue eyes. He told him that he and Maggie wanted him to come live with them.

Joseph rarely saw anyone other than his mother or brother. Occasionally a "sitter" would be there only to spend most of her time drinking coffee and reading magazines.

Joseph seldom, if ever, had any interactions with a man. Consequently, he was fascinated by this kind gentleman kneeling and speaking to him. Unexpectedly, even Maggie was somewhat taken aback when she saw what a cute, little child he was. He wasn't a happy bubbly little boy; however, he was adorable with black curly hair and incredible blue eyes. He really didn't comprehend what Stan said or what was happening. Stan very gently asked, "Joseph, would you like to come with me?" Instinct told the little one to nod his head and he did.

Stan was fighting back tears when he placed his hands on Joseph's tiny shoulders as he asked, "Okay, ready?" Joseph slightly nodded his little head again while staring into Stan's beckoning eyes.

Then Stan bent down even farther and scooped Joseph up in his arms and held him so close that for the first time in this little boy's life, Joseph felt the security and tenderness of love. He still didn't smile. His tiny heart was beating fast and even though he was unaccustomed to being hugged, he put his delicate pint-size arms around Stan's neck. A connection between the two was one that neither had ever experienced. This little innocent child had put a stirring inside Stan so touching that he could hardly speak. He managed to mumble a 'thank you' to Georgina as she handed Maggie a bag of Joseph's belongings.

Georgina's son watched his mother from the safety of strong comforting arms. He did not reach out for her, or cry for her, when Stan carried him out of the only home he had ever known and into a new life. Joseph couldn't take his eyes off of Stan, and Stan couldn't take his arms from around Joseph. Stan told Maggie that she would have to drive the car home even though she didn't have a license. He just couldn't stop holding his '*son*' against his chest. He didn't ever want to let go of him, and Joseph wasn't ready to let go of Stan either.

Stan took his new role as father seriously. He was chief cook and bottle washer during the day while Maggie worked at Hudson's. Georgina never asked Maggie about Joseph and that set well with Maggie. Stan was working the night shift. When he left for work in the evening, Maggie would be in charge of the baby. She did not take to motherhood very well. She would put Joseph in a playpen that was only a few inches off the floor and had high wooden slats all the way around. Joseph didn't mind the playpen even though it doubled as his bed.

Maggie, Joseph's new **mother**, would fix him a cup of warm milk around 6:30 PM. After drinking his milk cocktail, which included part of a dissolved sleeping pill, he slept until morning when his daddy would be home from his conductor job at the train station. Maggie told her doctor she needed sleeping pills at night; she did need them, though, not necessarily for herself.

Years seemed to fly by and little Joseph was growing quickly. In spite of his mother's neglect, he was becoming a handsome young man with a beautiful head of black curly hair and extraordinary blue eyes. In his preteen years he was a good student at the Catholic academy. He was tall and straight with a strong name, Joseph Eugene Graham. Of course, almost everyone called him Joe, which he liked. When someone teased him and used his middle name and called him *Genie*, he hated it. He felt Genie was a girly name and would put up his fists, set a stance and prepare to fight whenever he heard it.

Now in his early teen years, Joe was somewhat of a loner. On a particularly beautiful autumn day, Joe was enjoying the walk home from school. He could feel the soothing warmth from the sun on his back. The sunlight behind him was throwing his shadow ahead of him. The air was cool and fresh. The leaves had turned from green into gold, red, and orange. He liked the rustling sound he made as he shuffled through the leaves. He was careful not to scuff up his shoes because that could mean a whack across the face from his mother.

Joe liked autumn. The muted colorful leaves and temperatures dropping meant change. Now that the trees were nearly bare, there was little in the way between him and the heavens. He could see white billowing clouds adrift in the clear blue sky.

Suddenly, he heard a flock of Canadian geese headed south to a warmer climate. They were flying in their spectacular Vee formation. He stopped to watch them and listen to the honking sounds they made as they vigorously flapped, flapped high overhead. Joe had read in a National Geographic magazine that the geese in the back honk the loudest encouraging the leader to continue, to keep going, persevering, on their purposeful journey. He stood watching until the birds were a small distant shadow. He drew in a breath to smell the faint odor of burning leaves that was subtly hanging in the air.

Joe continued to make crunching noises through the fallen leaves until he reached the apartment building where he lived. He opened the heavy outside door and walked up two flights of well-worn carpeted stairs. Opening the door to their apartment, he was surprised to find his parents sitting in the living room. It was rare that they were both home at the same time on a weekday afternoon. His mother was sitting in the green-striped chair in the living room still dressed in her Hudson's attire - skirt, blouse, hose and heels. *Why wasn't she at work?* His dad was wearing his railroad uniform as he stood looking out the window onto the street. He seemed to be in deep thought.

There was an unusual atmosphere in the room. A mood or feeling Joe didn't recognize. Stan and Maggie looked at him with apprehension at exactly the same time. Maggie held in her hand what looked like a legal document. ***What could be this be about?*** Stan spoke first. "I want to explain what has happened that will probably change our lives. My mother's sister, the one I called my Aunt Mamie, lived in Maple Rapids. She died suddenly of a stroke." Stan cleared his throat and continued, "She had a long-standing feud with her family and in a last hateful act, she left her immediate family out of her will." Aunt Mamie had legally bequeathed everything to Stan! As a result, he had inherited her farm including a house, barn, tool shed, chicken coop, seven cows, three pigs, several chickens, one rooster and a couple of aging horses. A farm hand named Al was doing the chores and keeping things going until Stan could see his way clear to take over. Joe leaned in towards where Stan was standing. He was trying hard to make sense of his dad's words.

Maggie was taking a long drag from her ever-present cigarette while mulling over the possibility of farm life. She had always lived in Detroit and enjoyed the hustle and bustle.

Stan on the other hand had been raised on a small farm near Midland, Michigan. He had been to his Aunt Mamie's farm many times. He had always helped with the haying as soon as he was old enough to use a pitch fork. He didn't exactly hate farm life, nevertheless, he was eager to move to the city when he landed the job as a train conductor in Detroit. To qualify for that position, he had passed a psychological test, a physical and an eye exam.

As a young man the physical was not a problem for Stan as he was a healthy, strapping farm boy. The mental test was primarily based on common sense, which he had plenty of and passed. The eye exam, unfortunately, was a different type of challenge. It was necessary to read the eye chart on the far wall *without glasses*. Stan was nervous and beads of sweat were beginning to form on his forehead because he knew he could not pass the eye test without his glasses. He needed them to see at a distance and that eye chart was at a distance. The applicants were lined up to read the letters and numbers on the black and white chart. He was in third in line when the first candidate read the chart aloud; as the next young man in line read the chart aloud, Stan got an idea. He could memorize the sequence of letters and numbers, then when it was his turn, he would recite from memory pretending to read them. He would need to hear the letters and numbers several times before it was his turn to pull this off.

He faked a cramp in his left leg and limped out of line. He grimaced, stretched and straightened his leg a few times, walked a step or two and took his place behind everyone else. This time he put himself last in the group. Now he could hear the chart read aloud many times. When it was finally his turn, he took off his glasses, looked at the chart and from memory said, *"0, p, b, 7, y, 3, w, r, 8"* and put his glasses back on. He had passed the eye test and started training for his new job the following week. A real accomplishment for a man with little formal education.

Stan moved from his parents' farm into a small boarding house which was a short walk to the train station. The other boarders complained of too much noise being so close to the tracks, but for Stan the rumbling trains with horns blasting was music to his ears. He had a job, wore a uniform and received a steady paycheck. Life was good.

Now nearly twenty years had passed and he was considering the possibility of moving back to farm life. He was trying to weigh the options. Having his own farm would be a lot different than working on someone else's place. Just then Maggie sashayed by him with her dark hair all done up on top of her head. She was clicking as she walked because she was breaking-in her new high heeled shoes. Stan didn't bother to look at her. He had some serious thinking to do. She didn't like it when he didn't notice her. She knew he was in deep thought about his aunt and her farm. That farm was now his responsibility.

Maggie sat down and lit yet another cigarette. She leaned her head back and blew out a puff of smoke in the shape of a circle and then broke the silence. She told Stan she would go to that god-forsaken hellhole filled with animals and manure, if he promised to sell it as soon as he fixed it up and could get a good price for it. All she could see were dollar signs and a nice little bank account. Stan was somewhat surprised though pleased that she would quit her job and move with him. He agreed, when the economy was better, he would consider selling his aunt's farm.

What Maggie wasn't telling him was that she had been caught in the storeroom on the third floor of Hudson's with her pants down along with the young stock boy, Wayne, whose pants were also down. Her coworker, Wayne, was carefully trying to put away some new stemware without breaking any of it, when Maggie slipped in looking for a certain pattern of crystal martini glasses. She came up from behind and reached around him in a most suggestive move that at first, he didn't know what she was doing. He wasn't naive and soon returned her attention. When a delivery man opened the stockroom door, he surprised the amorous couple and himself as Maggie and Wayne were panicking and trying to put their clothes back on. Rumors were spreading through Hudson's like hot lava about Maggie and the stock boy. She was feeling that it might be time to leave Detroit, and Aunt Mamie's farm several miles from the city might be the answer … at least for now.

Joe wasn't even considered in the decision. He was never included in family matters. He just existed one day at a time. Stan quit his job at the train station and Maggie quit her job at Hudson's telling them that she and her husband had inherited an estate upstate. The three of them packed and moved to the farm.

Joseph enrolled in Maple Rapids High School where he was one of twenty-six freshmen. It was the assumption of the times that farm kids didn't need schooling. They were needed on the farm. They could learn everything they needed to know in the hayfields, gardens, barns and chicken coops. So, when Joe showed up for class wearing his Catholic academy dress code - a white shirt, black knickers, black socks and polished black shoes, he was laughed at, made fun of and beat up. When Maggie asked him why his clothes were so dirty and bloody, he told her that the kids teased him, bullied him and taunted him to fight.

When he told his mother that he needed different clothes so he could look like the other kids, she kicked him hard in his shin and said, "Just because we live on a farm doesn't mean you are going to dress like a damn hillbilly. You'll wear the school clothes we bought you. You'll wear what you've always worn. You dumb stupid ass." Maggie was not adapting well. She definitely missed bus service.

It was a long hard year for Joe. He soon gave up trying to fit in at school. Lunchtime was never easy with no one to eat with or talk to. He ate the hard-boiled egg and biscuit he brought each day, while standing by the coat rack. If someone walked by, he would pretend to be looking for something he left in his jacket pocket. He never made a friend, he was ignored or laughed at most of the time. At least the fights stopped.

Maggie wasn't fitting into her new environment much better. Knitting and quilting bees were not anything she would give any thought to joining. She said she was lonely and would take long walks in the woods. She would say that she needed some fresh air and would wander off out of sight. She would often be gone for a couple of hours. One Saturday afternoon, Joe was curious and decided to follow her as she slipped into the woods behind the row of fir trees in back of the milk house.

It was warm and pleasant that day and he could use some fresh air too. As he let curiosity get the best of him, he followed her. His mother's walks turned out to be clandestine meetings with Gerald Sommers, the man who owned the big farm down the road. Joe hid in the brush and watched while Gerald and Maggie greeted each other with an embrace. Mr. Sommers took off his sweaty work shirt and spread it on the ground under the shade of a Maple tree. He took Maggie's hands and led her to where his shirt made a place for her to sit. They talked quietly for a few minutes and that's when Mr. Sommers spit out his chewing tobacco, sat down beside Joe's mother, and pulled her to him. He then kissed her with his mouth open.

Joe felt sick as he watched his mother kiss him back. She unbuttoned her blouse and raised her skirt to reveal that she wasn't wearing any underwear. They were fondling each other when she got on all fours. She let Mr. Sommers mount her like a bull in the field mounts a cow. *How could she let that smelly lecherous man, who probably hadn't had a bath in a week, do that to her?* They seemed so familiar with each other that Joe knew this must be a regular event. He took off running back towards their farm and Stan. He saw his dad plowing with his team of two old horses. Their names were Ruby and Pearl. They were Stan's jewels. As a matter of fact, Stan loved all the living things on his farm. How could Joe possibly tell Stan what he had seen? How could he hurt the person he loved more than anyone or anything?

Last week, while he and Joe were mending a fence row, they were startled by a big, ugly snake slithering by. Joe raised his shovel to chop off the creature's head when Stan stopped him just in time to save its life. Stan spoke softly to the snake and told it to be on its way. Stan knew Michigan had poisonous rattlers, thankfully, this one wasn't a Massasauga. The snake presented no threat except to the rodent population which the snakes kept under control. He told Joe not to kill it. He explained, "It was just doing what God meant it to do – it was being a snake."

Joe had every intention of telling his dad what he had seen his mother and Mr. Sommers doing in the woods this afternoon, except it was hard to do. His dad was such a nice man and so good to him that he just couldn't bear to see him hurt. He watched while his dad wiped his brow with the sleeve of his dusty shirt, and then he filled a bucket with water from the pump in the yard and took the bucket to give Ruby and Pearl a long, cool drink. He then took a drink himself from the same pail. Joe loved this man so much that he just couldn't say anything about Mr. Sommers. Joe valued Stan too much to tell him something so disgusting. It would have to wait.

Joe saw his mother come in from her walk in the woods smoking a cigarette and humming a little tune. He followed her into the kitchen and under his breath he said, "I know what you do in the woods with Mr. Sommers, and I'm going to tell Dad."

Maggie snarled at him and grabbed an iron skillet. She raised it to hit him, but Joe was quick to seize her wrist and the heavy skillet fell to the floor with a bang and a loud thud. Stan was just coming up the back steps and asked what the commotion was all about. Joe and Maggie stood glaring at each other while Stan bent down and picked up the skillet. Maggie bellowed, "Your son is a clumsy fool."

"Don't worry," he said not looking at either of them. "The pan looks okay. Everything's fine." Stan was very aware of the tenseness in the air and chose not to ask what had happened. He had already decided that he didn't have the skills or knowledge to sort out the problems between his wife and his son.

To throw attention from the incident, Maggie announced that Joe's Aunt Georgina and his cousin Harold were going to pay them a visit on Sunday. Joe had met them twice before and wasn't impressed. They were stiff and hard to talk to. Aunt Georgina was small and reserved while his cousin Harold ignored him when he tried to start up a conversation. Harold would never want to play catch out in the yard or try to jump the ditch between the house and the road. He was a bore. He was a city kid. No one had ever bothered to tell Joe that Aunt Georgina was not his aunt but that she was actually his biological mother and that Harold was not his cousin, he was Joe's older brother.

Joe would have to put off telling his dad about Mr. Sommers. Of course, Maggie knew now that Joe was aware of her sneaky little fun walks with Gerald Sommers. So what, she thought! *Joe needed to learn about life and that there was more in the world than milking cows and gathering eggs.*

Joe's eighteenth birthday gave Maggie a reason to invite some friends over for a little party. She loved to dance. Not much dancing was happening at the farm. She often danced by herself waltzing around the living room while smoking a cigarette and humming an old tune. She invited a few families from neighboring farms for a social gathering using Joe's birthday as the reason.

Stan went out into the yard and chased the chickens until he caught one. He gripped its feet in one hand and held it so its head was on the chopping block creating easy access to its neck. He quickly raised the axe with his free hand and in a matter of seconds the headless chicken was running around in circles until it finally dropped.

The guests ate fried chicken that Stan prepared. The salads and desserts were whatever guests brought with them to add to the meal. Stan and Joe cleared the dining room by pushing the heavy oak table in the corner and placing the spindle-back dining room chairs against the wall so people could sit or dance.

Almost everyone danced the night away while drinking sweet dandelion wine made in Mr. Sommers' cellar.

Maggie was in charge of the dance floor. She grabbed every guy young and old and seductively swayed to the beat of the music. She was a little drunk on Gerald's wine when she coaxed Joe onto the dance floor with her. He really didn't know how to dance. Secretly, he did want to learn in case he had the chance to go to one of the Friday night barn dances in Maple Rapids. Almost everyone around there went every week. Joe didn't go because he couldn't dance. He heard pretty girls attended the barn dances, so maybe, he thought he should let Maggie teach him how.

When a nice slow melody started playing, Maggie took the opportunity to pull Joe onto the makeshift dance floor. "Come on Joe . . . *baby*," she teased in an all too seductive voice. She grabbed his hand and placed his right arm around her waist while she threw her left arm around his neck. She pushed her body much too close to his and started to sway back and forth moving her feet in small sliding steps. Joe was uncomfortable having her body rubbing against his. As he tried to pull away, his mother put her thigh between his legs and together they moved across the room in time to the music. She was brushing his crotch with each move and almost touching his privates with her leg. Against everything he knew was right, his body betrayed him and he was feeling aroused. When she realized what was happening and saw the panic in his eyes, she threw her head back and laughed a triumph laugh.

Joe shoved her away from him, rushed out of the room and ran upstairs to the safety of his bedroom. Joe slammed the rickety bedroom door shut and stood there trying to gather his thoughts. His room's decor had never been a priority. Old wallpaper with faded yellow flowers was peeling off the walls and the window sill, that had been painted white years ago, was also peeling. No one seemed to notice the deterioration of the room. The double bed was creaky with a lumpy mattress. There was a small chest of drawers beside the bed. A few hooks were nailed on the back of the door to hang clothes.

He paced the little room back and forth in the dark for a very long time. Finally, the music from downstairs stopped and he heard guests leaving. As the last person said goodbye, the sound of his mother coming up toward his room was getting louder. She was a little unsteady from all the wine she drank when she crudely, without knocking pushed open his door and stood there smoking a cigarette.

Joe was furious and shouted, "What were you doing? For god sake! You're my mother!" Still smirking, she came close to where he was standing. He felt unsteady and was trembling with anger. She came closer and he could smell alcohol on her tobacco breath along with her sweaty body odor that was mixing with too much cheap perfume. He felt ill.

She blew a puff of cigarette smoke in his face and snarled, "You damn fool. I'm not your mother! Ha! You stupid kid. Stan's not your father either." Tears were forming in Joe's eyes. She choked a little on her own cigarette smoke as she lied saying, "The only reason you're here is because Stan couldn't give me a child of my own so he adopted you. Look at you. You're crying like a feeble-minded idiot. No wonder your birth mother gave you away. She didn't want you!"

Maggie took a long drag from her cigarette, blew the smoke toward the ceiling, picked a bit of tobacco from her tongue, and left him to his misery. She didn't slam the door as she exited. She didn't need to . . . she already felt victorious.

Joe's hands were covering his ears as he closed the door with his back. He realized he hated her and always had. She was cruel. When he was a child, she would strip him naked and whip him with a belt for spilling a glass of milk or for falling asleep at the kitchen table. She would call him names and refer to him as good for nothing. She often liked to tell him that he was as useless as nipples on a bull.

Maggie was not his mother! He was trying to let it sink in. He was relieved and confused at the same time. He was feeling a little dazed as he dealt with this information.

"GOOD," under his breath, he whispered. "She isn't my real mother."

Chapter 5

CHASING LOVE

Joseph woke up to the sound of mooing cows asking to be relieved of their full udders. He heard Stan up early making a pot of coffee and getting ready to start chores.

The coffee aroma filtered up through the floorboards. He knew Stan was stirring a spoonful of sugar and a splash of fresh cream into his cup of strong hot coffee. Joe quietly dressed into his tee shirt and overalls, then slipped down the stairs and into the kitchen where Stan was sitting at the table with a cup in his hand. Joe wondered how much of the conversation Stan heard last night. His confrontation with Maggie had been brutal.

As he watched Stan prepare for a full day of hard work on the waiting farm, he felt such compassion for his dad. He was looking at the man who had raised him as his own flesh and blood; this man who worked so hard and was the only person he ever really loved. Joe was not looking forward to asking the question he had to ask, but he had to know if he were Stan's real son. Trying not to show any emotion, Joe looked at the cup in Stan's hand, because he couldn't look at Stan's face, and asked him point blank, "Am I your son?"

Without any hesitation, Stan took the last sip of his coffee and said, "Yes" and went out the back door, pulled on his work boots and headed for the barn.

Joe sat down at the kitchen table wondering what to do. He waited ten minutes until he knew Stan would be sitting on the wooden milk stool with a pail under the cow to catch its milk. Each of the four barn cats would be on alert as Stan would point the cow's teat at one of them and the cat would stand on its hind legs to catch a quick squirt of milk in its mouth. Each cat knew the routine and would watch for a turn. Joe walked into the barn just as the little Calico was smacking her lips.

Joe stood on the opposite side of the cow from where Stan sat on a stool milking. He didn't want eye contact when he said, "Mother told me you and she aren't my real parents." Somewhere in Joe's heart he knew, even before Stan spoke, that it was true.

Stan squeezed the cow's teat freeing its milk into the bucket and said, "As far as I'm concerned you are my son and you always will be. You mean more to me than any man's son ever meant to him. It is true that I wasn't given you through Maggie. I thought I would never be able to call anyone my son." He hesitated and continued, "No, Maggie and I couldn't have children, so God stepped in and gave me you - a son of my own. Yes, you are my son by the grace of God. Yes, Joe, you are my son!"

To keep himself from showing his emotions, Stan whistled and one of the cats came out of nowhere for another warm squirt of fresh milk.

Joe was confused. He was letting what Stan said sink in. He sat down on the nearest bale of hay and was silent. The only sound for several minutes was the ping, ping, ping of the cow's milk hitting the tin pail.

Joe finally stood and said, "Thank you, I want you to know that whatever happens, I love you as a son loves his dad. They taught us at Saint Francis that God has a plan for our lives. I . . . I think maybe He did mean for me to be with you."

Joe rarely saw Stan cry, even on the day when he had to take care of his workhorse, Ruby. She had stepped in a hole, broke a leg, and couldn't get up. The plow horse was old and something had to be done as she was suffering. Stan went into the house and came out with his shotgun. One shot to the head put his old pal out of her misery. When Joe and Stan finished digging a hole on the nearest edge of the field, Stan harnessed up Pearl and tied one end of a rope to her and the other end to Ruby's carcass. Pearl, with the help of Joe and Stan, pulled her best friend, Ruby, to her awaiting grave. With each shovel of dirt Stan threw on top of his faithful horse, he squinted and screwed up his face to keep back the tears that were so dangerously trying to escape. Stan thought if he let these tears flow now, he may never be able to stop them. He had held tears back all his life. They'd flood the field if he ever let them go.

33

It was time for Stan to buy a little tractor. He had been putting it off as he loved plowing with his two aging horses. Walking behind Ruby and Pearl tilling the soil, turning up fresh smelling earth, always made him feel close to God. His very soul was at peace when he and the "girls" were plowing.

When Stan and Joe went into the house that afternoon, Maggie said, "Look at you two. All sad and gloomy over a damned ol' nag that didn't know any better than to break her damn leg."

Joe was at such loose ends. He must have biological parents out there somewhere, but where? He was torn between trying to find them or just letting it go. After all, they obviously didn't want him. He wanted to think that they at least thought about him sometimes. Were they dead? Who were they?

Joe needed space . . . to sort things out. He needed time to digest all of this. He would graduate high school next week. He knew better than to make any quick decisions. His brain was feeling like mush. He needed to get away from the farm and think.

Joe started walking down the driveway towards the dusty road. When he reached the road, he turned left and just kept walking with no destination planned. He walked a little over three miles until he came to Sweet Meadows.

Sweet Meadows was a little group of homes and businesses. There was no traffic light, only a four-way stop. The little town was called Sweet Meadows because of the wonderful fragrance that came from the wild flowers and trees that surrounded the area. It was always a blessing to leave the manure-smelling farms and come into Sweet Meadows. The four corners consisted of a small hardware store that doubled as a drug store, Jake's Diner offering home cooking and a pool table, Smittie's Grocery was on another corner, and the last corner had the only gas station for miles around.

The Sweet Meadow's gas station was owned and operated by Hazel Mac. Joe had to chuckle to himself as he remembered her husband, Arnold Mac, who had run the place for 19 years. The story goes while pumping gas for Ginger Stamm, Arnold grabbed his chest, dropped the hose, fell to the ground and died. Ginger Stamm was known as the town's pin-up girl. She had full, large breasts that she displayed proudly. Her blouses were either too low and revealed too much flesh or they were too tight and emphasized what was underneath. She bleached her hair, wore bright red lipstick, and painted her long finger nails the same shade of red. Ginger fashioned herself from the cover of a magazine she saw in the drug store/hardware store. It was a trashy publication called "Sassy Sis".

No one blamed Ginger, the pin-up girl, for Arnold Mac's death - but talk was that those red lips and luscious breasts were just too much for his weak functioning heart to take. Ginger never really got over seeing someone die right before her eyes. She hadn't even offered to help him. She just watched through her new rhinestone studded dark sunglasses as he lay on the ground drawing his last breath.

Joe recalled the few days following Arnold's death. He remembered attending the funeral. Ginger "the pin-up girl" had put on a black dress and was there to pay her respects. The black dress was much too revealing for a funeral as it had a plunging neckline and was at least a size too small. The fit was snug. Along with her black stockings and three-inch pumps, she commanded a lot of attention. It was miraculous that none of the other men suffered the same fate as Arnold Mac since each man caught his breath when she slunk by. More than one man got an elbow in the side from his wife if he seemed to be watching Miss Ginger a little bit too intently.

Now, two years later, as Joe crossed the street, he waved to 'widow' Hazel Mac and went into Jake's Diner. He made himself comfortable on one of the stools at the counter. Just as he ordered a soda, the door opened and a handsome young man entered. He looked to be about twenty-five. He nodded and smiled at each one of the patrons. Everyone in Sweet Meadows that day seemed fascinated to see such a striking figure of a man. He was wearing a "sailor suit". He was perfection from the top of his head to the tip of his highly-polished shoes. For sure, he wasn't a 'local.'

Joe soon found out that this stranger was a naval recruiter. He had pamphlets showing a magnificent ship equipped with impressive wartime guns jetting out from its sides. The ship was being pictured on beautiful balmy seas floating off to Utopia carrying a squad of fresh, smiling, fit-looking sailors.

A bolt of lightning seemed to hit Joe's brain. *He would join the Navy and see the world from a massive warship.* He was no longer wondering what to do with his life. He knew! It was crystal clear. He would become a sailor for the United States of America. It felt right.

He followed the immaculate-looking recruiter out of Jake's Diner and without hesitation asked, "How can I join?" The recruiter put his arm around Joe's shoulders and introduced himself as Stephen. "Well, as long as you're at least eighteen years old, can pass a physical and don't have any warrants for your arrest, you could probably join as soon as next week."

Stephen knew that if he ended their conversation there, he might easily lose this young man's interest. So, he offered to drive Joe back to his home and speak with his parents. Joe declined, "I do not need parental permission." He didn't want Stan or Maggie involved. He just wanted to board that ship he saw in the picture and sail away to ports unknown . . . as far away from Maple Rapids as possible.

Stephen escorted Joe over to his official car. The two sat in the front seat and filled out papers. They set up a day and time for Joe to go to Midland and be tested and given a physical. Stephen picked up on Joe's hesitation and asked, "Is there a problem with getting to Midland next Tuesday morning?"

Joe nodded his head yes and spoke, "I have no transportation."

Stephen knew he had a live one on his hook and besides he really liked Joe. Stephen asked, "How about I pick you up here at Jake's Diner on Tuesday at 7:00 AM? It would be my pleasure to transport you to the naval office in Midland."

Joe had very little interaction with Maggie or Stan in the few days that led up to Tuesday morning. He was so excited. He was a little worried about oversleeping and not being at Jake's by 7:00 AM. Sometimes he slept through the rooster crowing at dawn . . . so he drank close to a gallon of water before he went to bed Monday night, making sure he would have to get up early to relieve himself. It worked.

It was not quite light when Joe quietly dressed and tiptoed down the creaky stairs and out the kitchen door. He walked at a very fast pace down the driveway, turned left onto the road and walked three miles into Sweet Meadows where at 6:45 AM Stephen was waiting for him in front of Jake's. He was in his official car, dressed flawlessly in his fine-looking uniform with his white cap slightly covering his forehead emphasizing his greenish colored eyes and perfectly shaped brows. He stepped out of his car and stood tall and straight until Joe was close enough for him to offer a white-gloved handshake.

The scene almost seemed unreal. Joe wanted to pinch himself to make sure he wasn't dreaming. Stephen looked like a celebrity and here he was giving his undivided attention to Joe. Stephen was treating Joe as though he was the "celebrity." Stephen seemed to glide as he went around to the other side of the car to open the door for Joe. Seeing that Joe was comfortable, he closed the door without slamming it, and did a strutted march to the other side of the car. He then repositioned himself behind the steering wheel. Stephen had neither smiled nor frowned, he just had a pleasant look on his face that indicated he was in control of the situation.

Once they reached the Midland offices, Stephen accompanied Joe into a holding room where about twenty other young men were waiting for physicals and shots. Joe had no problem with the physical and passed the academic testing.

Joe was sworn in as a naval cadet.

Chapter 6

FINDING LOVE

*I*t was late when Joe arrived back at the farm. Maggie and Stan had already turned in for the night. He was quiet, not wanting to wake them as he went into the kitchen to grab a slice of bread and a hunk of cheese. An uneasy feeling came over him when he went upstairs and entered his bedroom. He sat down on the side of his lumpy mattress and tried to identify what he was feeling.

The stirring within him was likely to be apprehension mixed with excitement. After a few minutes it came to him. He was feeling alive for the first time in a very long time. The odd sensation in the pit of his stomach was good, really good. Joe woke early the next morning. His feet hit the floor before the old rooster crowed. He ran down the stairs to join Stan for a quick breakfast of oatmeal laced with butter and brown sugar. He cooled his cup of steaming coffee with thick cream and drank it quickly without really tasting it.

He was eager to get on with his life. He was due in Midland at the recruiting center Monday at 8:00 AM. A bus load of new recruits was being transported to the Great Lakes Naval Station in Lake County, Illinois. He would soon be training at that naval boot camp.

Stan and Joe milked the cows, fed the animals and gathered the eggs. They put the cows out to graze and cleaned up the stanchions. When they went inside the house to wash up and have a bite to eat at noontime, Joe stuttered and stammered when he told Stan that he had decided to join the Navy. Stan looked up from the apple he was slicing with his pocket knife. He silently stared at Joe as he held a slice of the apple between his thumb and the blade of his knife. He put the apple slice in his mouth, crunched on it and with some of the apple still in his mouth, he asked, "How soon?"

Joe looked into the only eyes that had ever looked at him with love and said, "Monday."

Stan stood up, leaned over and lightly rested his hand on Joe's shoulder. "I wish you well, son. God's blessing. You will be missed here."

Joe stood and put out his right hand for Stan to shake it. Stan looked down at Joe's hand and started to take it, then instead roughly took Joe in an embrace. When Stan regained his composure and stepped back, Joe asked, "Will you tell *her* that I'm leaving?" Stan nodded his head that he would tell Maggie. Tears were starting to careen down his rugged, weathered face getting caught in the lines that crisscrossed his leathery cheeks.

Stan didn't want to stand in the way of Joe having a life away from the farm. The unpleasant thought of living without him made Stan feel weak in the knees. For a moment he thought he might lose his balance. The years he watched Joe grow from a fragile little, neglected toddler into a vigorous young man was the only thing that had made living with Maggie bearable. Now he was losing Joe.

Stan asked, "Can I do anything to help you with whatever needs to be done?"

Joe responded by saying, "I need a ride to Midland on Monday morning. The bus leaves for the naval station in Illinois at 8:00 AM sharp."

Stan said, "Okay. I'll drive you. It's the least I can do for you after everything you have done for me."

"Me? Me done for you?" questioned Joe. "I haven't done much of anything for you."

"Oh no, Son, without knowing it you taught me what love is - what it's like to look at someone and feel your heart soar - what it's like to care so much that you would willingly lay down your life for someone." Joe couldn't even look at Stan. He just couldn't let anything stand in the way of his leaving.

When Monday morning arrived, Stan asked if Joe wanted to say goodbye to Maggie. Joe shook his head and said, "Just let her sleep, okay?"

Stan started the car and pulled out of the driveway. Maggie woke when she heard the car start up. She raised up just in time to see them drive away. She felt nothing. Joe was much too aware of her appetite for men who weren't her husband. She lay back down and fell asleep even though the morning sun was up and beginning to brighten the room.

As Stan and Joe pulled into the Midland naval recruiting parking lot, they saw a large bus in the very back behind the building. The doors were open and young men with suitcases and bags were standing by waiting to load.

Joe looked at Stan and said, "This is it. Thanks, Dad. I want you to know I will keep in touch with you no matter what. I'll let you know how you can reach me."

That said, Stan and Joe got out of the car together and walked around to the back to get Joe's canvas bag from the trunk. As Stan lifted open the trunk, Joe reached in and slowly pulled out his bag. The two looked each other in the eye and shook hands not feeling comfortable to hug in public. Joe turned and walked over to join the group gathering beside the bus.

Stan didn't move other than to slam the trunk down. He stood in the damp morning air watching his son disappear into the interior of the bus which was quickly filling. The recruits were in a hurry to get inside, eager for their new beginnings.

Stan still didn't move from behind his car. He felt like his boots were glued down. He watched until the bus pulled away. It was soon out of sight with its load of hopeful, bright-eyed future sailors. Stan would take the long way home to delay interaction with Maggie. He didn't know how he could live with her without Joe.

Inside the bus it was relatively quiet considering all the young energetic passengers. The only stop was a restroom break in Benton Harbor before reaching their destination.

When the bus arrived at the naval boot camp, the recruits were ushered into the mess hall for a spaghetti dinner, with salad, garlic bread and chocolate cake, coffee and milk. Just as the last of the cake was being eaten, three naval officers entered. They were handsome, well-groomed men and made quite a first impression. When one of them asked for attention, the building went silent. Another officer told the men to check the bulletin boards outside the doors that led into the hallway. On the boards were posted names of all the recruits and their assigned barracks where they would live while in training.

The camp's thirty-nine buildings were built between 1905 and 1911. The base was like a small city with its own fire department, naval security forces (police), and public works department all on 172 acres. The complex boasted of its clock tower and large parade grounds in front of the administration building. Recently new barracks, mess halls, classrooms and staff offices at the training center were built for around $8,000,000. During WWII over one million sailors were trained at this compound.

Joe's barracks was clean and plain without privacy. Being raised an only child and not making friends easily, Joe was somewhat uncomfortable being with other men twenty-four hours a day. The basic training was strenuous but not tortuous for a tough farm kid. He didn't stand out but kept up with the best of them. When things got rough, he focused on the beautiful ship sailing off to parts unknown on heavenly, sparkling blue waters.

He sent short letters home to Stan letting him know that he was doing okay and that he was preparing for the naval excursions. When the training was completed, he would then be assigned to a warship. Joe received an even shorter letter back from Stan telling him that everything was fine at the farm except he found his old horse, Pearl, down in the far north end of the field. She had just laid down and died of old age.

Joe had an uninvited thought, *"Too bad it hadn't been Maggie who just laid down and died of old age."*

Stan gave Joe a PO Box number to send future letters to because, he went on to explain, mail service wasn't always very good out at the farm. Joe knew the real reason for an alternate address was that Stan worried Maggie would intercept his letters. If Stan wasn't home to get the mail before she did, she might not let him know that Joe had written. Joe and Stan would correspond often. No long letters, just a line or two.

As his stint at the naval station was drawing to a close, Joe was excited to leave for an awaiting ship to take him away to a new life of adventure. His training and expertise were in the engine room. He didn't mind heights and he realized, thanks to the Navy, that he had an innate ability for wiring and electronics. If he decided not to make the military a career, he was well prepared to get a job as a lineman with an electric company or telephone company when his tour of duty with the Navy was over.

The graduation ceremony was full of pomp and circumstance with everyone in full dress uniform stepping in exact unison as the compound's orchestra was playing a Sousa march. Family and friends were in awe at the glamor of it all. Joe had no one there to share his special day. He hadn't even invited Stan. When the function was over, the sailors received their orders.

Joe was dumbfounded when he read his official papers. He was to leave the base via a transport plane and would report to the base on the Azores Islands until further notice. The command mission would be to support NATO (North Atlantic Treaty Organization) forces in the area, to assist in local defense (if requested) and to protect and evacuate United States citizens from the Azores, Europe, Africa, Southwest Asia and other areas of the world.

The Azores are a series of nine islands in the middle of the North Atlantic Ocean. They are located about 2,400 miles east of New Jersey and about 930 miles west of Portugal and are owned by Portugal. The main language of the island residents is Portuguese but, by necessity, most of the inhabitants are bilingual and speak English. The air force base at the Azores is an important mid-ocean refueling and pit stop for allies.

For the moment at least, it looked like Joe's dream of being on a ship would have to wait. The flight to the Azores on a transport plane was hot and uncomfortable. He was looking forward to getting there and getting some fresh air. When they landed and were led off the plane, he saw the islands for the first time and was somewhat surprised. The view was beautiful. There were gorgeous wild flowers, trees and beautiful mountains.

Two military supply trucks arrived and transported the sailors to their new home, another barracks. They were treated to a roast beef and mashed potato dinner with Neapolitan ice cream for dessert. They were given uniforms and instructions on how to care for those uniforms. Cleanliness and neatness were priorities. Joe liked the new uniforms. They made him feel like he fit in. He wore the same clothes as his peers, unlike the high school years that he spent being bullied about his clothing. He could and would get used to more barracks living and close quarters for eating and sleeping. It wasn't fun. He wouldn't have chosen it, but it was okay for a time until he could get on a ship and sail the seas.

After a few weeks of orientation and more training, he joined the football team for fun. There were Navy teams, Air Force teams, Army teams and a few others. Joe's team wasn't great but he enjoyed playing. For the first time he made friends, real buddies, real pals. Two of his teammates were also from Michigan. Bruce was from the Ann Arbor area and Lonnie from Milford. The three of them made up the strength of defense for their team. Lonnie was made center as he had been on his high school team. The three of them played hard. They were usually beat up and bruised by the end of a game and would go out drinking to ease their pains and wounded egos.

There were always women hanging around outside the base looking for a good time and a few dollars. These were not the kind of girls you would take home to meet the family. Joe, Bruce, and Lonnie were making life tolerable on the Azores. Joe was not interested in the females who went out and partied with all the guys. But he *was* interested in the little Portuguese girl who worked in the bakery of what everyone called town.

The little shops didn't have a real name, rather they were a group of small privately-owned businesses referred to as town. There was a food market, liquor store, open vegetable and fruit stands, and a gift shop/jewelry store. The jewelry store was busy because it was the only place service men and women could buy gifts and have them sent to loved ones back home.

At the edge of this grouping was a bakery that smelled like heaven must smell. The pastries and odors were not what brought Joe inside the little bake shop. It was the beautiful Portuguese girl who waited on him when he bought a sweet biscuit made of honey, flour, butter and nuts.

Joe went to the bakery every chance he had just to get a glimpse of her long black hair, delicate hands and shy smile that melted his heart. Joe longed for her to notice him but her dark eyes never fully met his gaze.

Of course, Bruce and Lonnie teased him unmercifully. To them she was just a cute little Portuguese girl who worked in the bakery, but to Joe she was an angel sent from heaven. He asked her name once and she said, "Isabel." When she said it out loud, to him, it sounded like an angelic choir was singing it. He longed to know her. He was even forgetting about the elusive, glamorous warship that would take him to ports unknown. He would rather look at Isabel than look at any of the seven wonders of the world.

Joe didn't know how he could approach her to let her know that he had fallen in love with her the first time he saw her. He had asked her name and she told him but she didn't respond by asking him his name or anything about him.

He knew all too well the GIs who would like a date with her just to neck and have a few beers. Joe's interest was not so shallow. He felt something much deeper in his heart when he was near Isabel. He felt a longing, NOT a lusting. He had noticed a necklace she always wore that held a gold cross. The cross fell about five inches below her slender, soft neck.

He had written Stan and told him all about her and Stan had written back promptly with his advice to *"not be shy - for if she were shy too, they would never get to know one another.*" On Stan's urging, Joe decided the next time he saw her, he would break the ice and get her to talk to him. He would ask her where she got the lovely necklace she always wore.

Joe worked up his nerve and stopped by the bakery just as Isabel was sprinkling vanilla cupcakes with red sugar chips that sparkled. Her finger tips were stained red from the dye in the red sprinkles. He pretended to be very interested in the cupcakes and when he looked up from them, he saw the gold cross dangling away from its usual resting place on her neck. He reached over for just a moment and touched the cross, then quickly leaned away.

"Where did you get that pretty necklace?" he asked in his friendliest voice.

"Oh, it is so old. My grandmother used to wear it. When she passed away, I asked if I could wear it and my mother said I could. I have part of my grandmother with me every day. She was the person who started our bakery. She started by baking bread and sugar cookies. You Americans loved it. So now here we are," Isabel explained in a bit of an accent as she sprinkled the last cupcake.

It suddenly dawned on Joe that he never had grandparents or at least never knew any. He dismissed that disturbing thought and focused on spending time with Isabel.

He just blurted out, "I want to see you and get to know you. I'm afraid you'll think I'm just like some of the other guys who aren't respectful. I promise you I will not say or do anything that might offend you."

Isabel looked down at her red fingertips and her vanilla cupcakes. She appeared to be thinking about what Joe had just said.

Finally, she looked up at Joe and said, "My parents are strict. There are always so many military men wanting girlfriends. The sailors go away and their girlfriends have babies a few months later. Some babies are black and Portuguese and some are white and Portuguese. Life is harder for those children and their families. Life is not easy here for my family and I don't want to make it harder for them by being with a GI. I'm sorry."

Isabel was the only girl Joe had ever been attracted to in this way. She was the only girl he had ever asked out. She was the only girl he would ever want to ask out, but she said, "No." He stared at her in disbelief. How could he feel this way about her and she not feel the same way about him? He stood in the bakery for a minute or two while she watched him deal with the rejection.

Isabel had refused many sailors but this was the first time she wished she could have accepted the invitation. He was handsome, of course, but she saw so much more in him than any of the others. He had a kindness, a sweetness, a gentleness. She was worried that he was the one she could fall for and then he would leave for a life away from the Azores and away from her.

Joe was so depressed that his letter to Stan that week was filled with gloom and doom. Stan's letter in return told him not to give up so easily. He said, "*Quitters never win. You want to win? Don't stop running before the race is over or you'll never win.*"

Joe needed to get away and think. Sometimes leaving the base and taking a walk in the open air had helped him lower his anxiety. The next day Joe felt the need to take a long walk. There was a path that led up the side of the mountain next to the naval compound. The Azores Islands were created by volcanos and got their name from *Azul* meaning "blue". Blue skies, blue waters and now Joe was going to try to walk his blues away.

His trek up that mountain path was just what he needed. He appreciated the beauty of nature and started to feel surrounded by its calming effect. After an hour of walking, he found a smooth ledge to sit on and took a drink of cool water from his canteen. The air was unpolluted and stimulating. He looked up at the clearest sky he had ever seen and asked God for help. He knew about God and could say the Rosary in his sleep but this was the first time he had spoken out loud to the Creator of the universe.

He felt such peace and even though he was a long, long way from people, he didn't feel alone. He thought he felt something brush his shoulder for just a moment. It was an unseen presence of something or someone. Joe felt moved and spoke out loud. He asked God to guide him. "If you are real, help me. Please urge Isabel to soften and give me a chance," he said prayerfully.

Joe came down from that mountain feeling better than he had felt in a very long time. When he went up that path, he wasn't expecting an encounter with the God he had only heard about in catechism, but he did. He went up that mountain alone but he would not be alone when he came down.

Joe knew the feeling of love. Stan had shown him love and Joe loved him back with all his heart. Joe had that feeling when he saw Isabel and now that same feeling of love engulfed him. The priest used to talk about God's love. Joe was feeling drenched by it. He breathed in new strength and breathed out old fears.

Chapter 7

TRUE LOVE

*B*efore moving to Maple Rapids, Joe had been raised in the Catholic faith, even serving as an altar boy while growing up in Detroit, but the closest he had ever been to God physically, mentally or spiritually was up on that awe-inspiring mountain. He had a feeling of peace, yet an excitement had flooded over him. The next time he saw Isabel, he would be able to give all he had toward making her feel the same way about him as he was feeling about her. He was determined to do whatever *he* could and God would just have to do the rest.

During his descent down the mountain, he saw beautiful blueish-purple flowers growing wild along the almost over-grown path. On his way up this mountain, his mind was in a blurred state and he had missed much of the lovely foliage. Now his mind was clear. He devised a plan that would start with flowers.

Joe knew Isabel and her family lived in a homemade bungalow that was an extension of their humble bakery. Due to his many walks around the place, he figured out which room must be Isabel's. It was a very small room, only about 8 x 9, but it was hers and it had a window with four small panes of glass. Well, three small panes of glass because one of the panes had been broken during a thunderstorm and had been replaced with a square of slightly warped plywood.

Early on a warm sunny morning Joe began his plan by propping a long-stemmed fragrant blueish-purple flower up against Isabel's window. He secured it with a stone. He left a note saying, *"This flower is a beautiful creation from God, but YOU outshine every blossom I have ever seen."*

Isabel was wiping the sleep from her eyes as she pushed open one side of her faded orange curtain when she saw the magnificent flower along with a piece of paper folded over twice. An excited quiver swept over her. She easily pushed the plywood out of the way and retrieved the flower and the note. She carefully put the lovely purple petals to her nose for a long inhale of their fragrance and then unfolded the note. She touched the note to her heart and knew who it was from. As she read what was written, she suddenly felt unworthy of his words. *Did he really find her to be beautiful?* Even though she was a naturally beautiful young woman, she was totally unaware of her attractiveness. No one had ever let her know.

She couldn't seem to get that handsome sailor out of her mind. She lived a sheltered life knowing little about romance and what went on between lovers. She had heard her parents in the next room moving around and making their bed squeak some nights. She knew somewhat instinctively what sex was but hadn't really been interested in learning much about it.

When she was thirteen or fourteen, a pimpled-faced teenage boy had come into the bakery to buy a pastry, and while paying for it, he had quickly shown her three small cards that looked like playing cards - but his cards were black and white pictures of a naked man and woman engaged in various sexual positions.

If those pictures were meant to excite her, they had the opposite effect. She stared at them for a moment while the young man smiled at her, obviously getting some perverted enjoyment out of watching her reaction. She just glanced up at him and without a word or a change in her demeanor, she handed him his fruit turnover. She then turned her back on him pretending to check one of the ovens and paid no more attention to the customer . . . thus giving him no satisfaction. She resumed her position at the counter as though nothing strange had happened, yet she never forgot her initiation into the world of pornography or the creepy guy with the cards.

Here and now, when she thought of Joe in her private moments, she felt a stirring in her body that was foreign to her. He was so handsome in his uniform. She felt a special kind of warmth and aching deep within her. This new sensation of arousal felt somewhat like having a butterfly caught up in her underpants.

The next morning, she quickly opened her curtain hoping to find another flower or another note. Only a note was there held safely in place with a stone. The note was from "a secret admirer." It said, *"Please meet me. Take the path that ends at the naval post and stay to the left. Just after you pass the rock wall, take twenty steps and turn right. I'll be waiting for you at 8:00 tonight."*

Her heart leaped under her thin cotton nightgown. She quickly dressed for work in gray slacks, white tee shirt and white gym shoes with no socks. The day in the bakery dragged and dragged. Her mother accused her of being distracted. Well, of course she was distracted, she couldn't stop thinking about the note. ***Should she go? Could she go? Would she go?***

Finally, it was 7:00 PM, and her father locked the front door of the bakery. A small supper was eaten of pan-fried fish, a few sautéed vegetables, two-day-old bread and custard pie left over from yesterday's fare. Their meager meal had been eaten and their tea sipped without a word of conversation. Isabel, her mother and her father just chewed quietly while looking down at their plates.

Isabel's heart was racing as she quickly helped clean up after their sparse meal. She tried hard to act casual when she told her parents, "It's such a beautiful evening, I thought I would just go for a walk and enjoy the wild flowers that are blooming everywhere." Her parents were completely exhausted from the hot, busy day and hardly looked up as she slipped out the back door.

She swiftly found the path that led to the base and then to the rock wall, then silently counted twenty steps moving her mouth with each number. When she mouthed twenty, she heard a man's voice say "twenty" out loud just as she took that 20th step. All of a sudden, she was being picked up off her feet and swung around in the air as Joe was smiling his biggest smile and laughing as he embraced her. His arms enfolded her and she felt a comforting safety she had never experienced before. He was so clean and warm. His strong arms around her brought a new feeling, it just seemed that she was right where she belonged.

When Joe finally let her feet touch the ground, he took her hands in his and kissed the palms of each of them. He placed her hands on his chest and took her head in his hands. He stood there staring down at her. His passionate blue eyes were holding her chocolate brown eyes captive. She felt like she was floating. *Was she dreaming?* He tipped her face up towards his and softly, ever so softly, put his lips on hers. She tried hard not to faint while everything within her was leaving earth. That tender kiss lasted a long time but she felt she must have another and another. In Joe's arms she found love.

She now understood sexual attraction and desire. Her small breasts were pressed against him and there was a heat growing between her legs. She could feel him harden as he held her close. Emotional tears were forming. She wanted him. She wanted to be with Joe all the way. If he had dared to ask her, she would have said, "Yes." Except he didn't ask. He held her without moving for a long time.

He gently pushed her away from him and looked longingly into her soft, gentle eyes searching for something to say. He finally just said, "I'll walk you home."

Joe wanted her so much that he thought of lying with her on the cool grass right then and there and making love to the only woman he had ever felt this way about. He fought the urge because he loved her so much that he just couldn't have sex with her and then have to leave her. He loved her too much to rush things. He wanted to want her after the love making and forever.

Since leaving the farm, Joe had been with a few women but after sex he didn't care if he ever saw them again. Isabel was different. He would never want to leave her side. *Would he feel the same about Isabel after the lovemaking was over?* No he would not.

She allowed him to walk her only partway back to the bakery. She did not want to take a chance of having her parents see her with a military man. Joe leaned to see her face and asked, "Can I meet your mom and dad sometime soon?"

Isabel frowned at the thought and said, "I would have to ask their permission."

"Then ask their permission," he said, "because *I* want to ask them for permission also."

She stopped walking and stared up at him. Her eyes were not blinking - just staring. "What are you saying?" she asked.

Joe turned to her and took her by the shoulders. He held her firmly but not tight enough to hurt her in any way, just forcefully enough so she knew he meant serious business. He said, "I want to marry you and I want your parents' blessings."

She looked down at the ground then lifted her questioning eyes to see him pleading with those extraordinary blue eyes of his. She couldn't move. She couldn't talk. She had a hard time breathing. Isabel slowly came to her senses and drew from a memory of her friend Rosie.

Rosie's life was ruined when she fell in love with a sailor guy who was sent to serve on a battleship for eighteen months. He was reassigned after that and Rosie never saw or heard from him again. The boys in the village shunned her as she was thought of as used goods. She now lived in the same village and took care of her sickly grandmother. At twenty-two years old Rosie's future looked pretty ugly, incredibly lonely. Isabel needed to be realistic. *Could this happen to her?*

As they neared her home, Isabel looked towards the back door of the bakery, then without a word went inside leaving Joe standing alone. He didn't know if he should run after her or let her have time to consider what he had just said to her. He gradually turned and slowly walked away.

Isabel did not sleep that night. She didn't eat the next day. She moped around the bakery and seemed to be going mindlessly through the daily ritual. That was all she knew to do. Her parents supposed that she was just experiencing teenaged moodiness or her time of the month and truthfully didn't pay much attention.

On the fourth day after the meeting with Joe, Isabel passed out cold in front of one of the hot ovens. Her mother wiped her hands with a nearby rag and hurried to her daughter. She knelt down and was worried when she saw Isabel's eyes were closed. However, she was more upset that the bread baking in that hot oven might burn. Isabel's mother called to her and shook her gently at first and then harder. Isabel moaned and opened her eyes slightly. Her mother took the opportunity to jump up and yank the six delicious smelling, crusty loaves of bread from the oven.

Isabel rolled to her hands and knees, crawled to the nearest chair and pulled herself to standing. When her mother saw her upright, she sputtered something and waved her away with her hands while resetting the temperature of the oven. Isabel stumbled to her room and fell sobbing onto her cot. She felt she couldn't fight it. The longing inside her for Joe was consuming her.

That evening supper consisted of soft-boiled eggs and rice, followed by dessert of day-old cinnamon rolls with butter and warm tea. Isabel tried to eat some rice. She was pale with dark circles under her eyes and her cheeks were dry and chafed from all the salty tears that had rolled down her face.

Her parents quickly caught a glimpse of each other's eye, but said nothing.

Isabel looked down at her plate, pushed the rice around with her fork and without looking up, blurted out, "I am in love with a sailor."

Her father threw his own plate across the tiny kitchen strewing food all over, while her mother seemed to turn into a pillar of stone. She did not move or say a word. She didn't cry or utter a sound.

Isabel's father got up from the table, stepped over his plate and the mess on the floor. He returned to the bakery where things made sense to him. Isabel kept her head down as she spoke to her mother, who still had not moved a muscle. "He wants to talk to you," Isabel whispered.

"No, No. Not ever!" her mother yelled.

"But Mama, he wants to marry me," Isabel pleaded

"Why would he want to marry a poor, skinny girl like you?" her mother sneered. "He is not one of ours. Do I have to remind you of what happened to Rosie? People call her nasty names, terrible names." Isabel's mother's nostrils were flaring as she spoke.

"This is different," wept Isabel. "This is different! He loves me," she said in her firmest voice.

Her mother finally stood and pointed her finger at Isabel and hissed, "You are a hussy, you are a dirty little girl . . . my daughter . . . a slut! A man from the base! No, oh no. You, you . . ." and then while shaking her head back and forth, she bent down and started to clean up the mess her husband had made with the supper she had prepared for him.

Her mother turned her back on Isabel in a meaningful gesture. Isabel knew that she would be disowned if she continued to see Joe. Her parents already thought of him as an evil man.

That night as she lay on her cot, Isabel was confused and depressed. Her thoughts were about possibly killing herself. Maybe she **WAS** a slut. Her desire for Joe was real. *Did that make her a slut? Would she let herself be a sailor's passing fancy?* She *could* end this unnerving clanging in her head by just jumping off a cliff into the sea!!! Yes, the accepting non-judgmental constant sea. The waves beckoning, always beckoning. She fell asleep, grateful for the silence in her mind. She awoke to a sound of light tapping on one of her window panes. She slipped off of her cot and looked out only to see Joe. He was tall and fit. His skin was shining and his hair was still wet from a recent shower. She stared out at him and knew without a doubt that she had to be with him no matter what people might call her. Joe was grinning as he motioned with his arms and hands for her to come and meet with him. They met at their same secret place in the wooded area off the main path. When Joe held her, he was concerned because she felt so thin and frail. "Are you okay?" he asked.

She whispered that she was fine. "Do you still want to marry me?" she asked.

He was taken by surprise. He backed away a little and looked intently at her.

"Yes, yes, yes, yes," he kept nodding his head, repeatedly saying yes until she put her hand over his mouth to stop the stream of yeses.

"Okay," Isabel said. "You will have to take care of whatever we need to do. We will not have permission from my parents, let alone their blessings, but I just turned eighteen and I'll be able to sign my own papers."

As soon as he left her, Joe went directly to the base chaplain who helped him with needed documents. Three weeks later the chaplain performed an informal ceremony and Isabel became Joe's wife.

Isabel never told her parents that she was now a sailor's wife, even though she spent many nights away from the bakery. Those nights were spent with her new husband on the beach. Joe had found a completely secluded area where there were some small caves that had been formed in the volcanic rock only a few yards from the water. Whenever he could get away from the base, he would signal her by placing a flower under a small stone on her window sill.

Isabel's parents barely spoke to her or to each other for that matter. She assumed they knew of her nights away from her little cot. Those were nights spent somewhere they didn't want to know about. So, they didn't ask.

Joe and Isabel loved to walk the beach barefooted in the warm sun or in the cool evenings under the stars. At the farthest deserted part of the beach the ground was stony instead of sandy. The stones never seemed to cause Isabel discomfort and she would find it funny and cute that Joe's feet were so pink and tender. He would often stop and slip on his shoes while she danced a little jig, showing off the bottoms of her feet that were like fine, smooth leather and just as tough.

They would swim and dry off on blankets provided by the US Navy and make love on a military sleeping bag in the privacy of their secret, secluded cave at the edge of the sea. Seven months after their marriage, Isabel missed her period. She wasn't nervous because she had often missed her monthly bleeding before she met Joe. Her female rhythm had always been a little off.

When she missed the next month also, she started to be a little concerned. Then she woke up in the middle of the night in her little room so sick that she barely made it to the toilet to throw up. The thought came to her that she might be pregnant.

She told Joe the news and explained how upset she was. After all, her parents didn't even know she was married. Joe smiled at hearing the news and held her tight. He put his hand on her tummy and spoke softly saying, "Hi, little one. I'm your papa." He picked Isabel up off the ground and swung her around and around in the air until he felt dizzy and she felt sick.

Joe had always kept in touch with his dad - well, the man he thought of as his dad, Stan. And right now, Stan was the one he wanted to talk to. He finally opened up to Isabel and told her of his upbringing and how he had left home because of the abusive woman who raised him. The woman he called '*Mother*.'

Joe was going to be a father. When his service time was over, he would take Isabel and his baby to the States. They could settle in New York or maybe California where jobs were plentiful, and live far, far away from his old life on the farm. He tried to put Maggie out of his thoughts with some success, but flashbacks of his so-called mother had a way of finding him in his dreams and in moments when he let his mind wander back to his youth. His entire adult life he kept himself busy, always filling his course with enough that there was little room left for images and reflections of his childhood.

He would quickly shut old memories out and flood his mind with thoughts of Isabel and her beautiful brown eyes. Those eyes that were surrounded by long black eyelashes, curled up so perfectly that they didn't look real. But nothing about Isabel was fake. Her skin was the color of pure maple syrup. He would often touch his lips to her cheeks, forehead, eyelids, chin and then to the warm soft lips that were waiting for his.

Isabel was going to have his baby!

Chapter 8

LOVE DIES, DIES, DIES

*I*sabel and Joe decided to call Stan together. Joe was laughing with delight when his dad answered the phone. Stan was almost delirious to hear from Joe. He explained in a weakening voice, "Joe, I need to tell you that Maggie died in a car accident in Atlantic City last week. She left me and was living with a former neighbor of ours. Maybe you remember Gerald Sommers? He didn't survive the accident either."

Joe couldn't really feel anything as he processed the news about his malicious "mother" and Mr. Sommers. He knew he should feel something, but all he could do was exhale a sigh of relief. The air suddenly seemed uncannily fresh. Maggie could no longer torment anyone. She was gone. Joe drew in another deep breath of clean refreshing air.

Stan continued, "I had to sell the farm. I couldn't keep things going. My back ain't what it used to be and my knees are pretty sore. I just needed a comfortable place to hang my hat and park my old car. I found a nice little house in Flint."

Both Stan and that old car had seen better days. He told Joe and Isabel that he was happy for them and, as soon as he moved, he would write them with his new address and phone number.

Their phone connection was lost before they had a chance to tell Stan that Isabel was "expecting". As they put the phone down, Isabel said, "Joe, you know you are so lucky to have a man in your life like Stan. I can't tell my own parents about our marriage let alone my pregnancy." She just didn't know what to do about that yet. She would need to tell them soon.

Isabel and Joe met at the beach the next night and the news from Joe was devastating. It was unthinkable. Joe was upset. He took her in his arms and said, "I'm being deployed, shipped out for eight months and there is nothing, nothing I can do about it. Orders are orders. I always dreamed about sailing the seas, but now there is no place I want to be if it means being away from you. I am so sorry. I will have to leave you for a while."

Isabel was hit hard. She didn't see this coming. He would leave her. She would have the baby without a husband anyone knew about.

She was falling into a deep depression, crying a lot and mindlessly blundering through her days at the bakery.

After Joe left on his ship, her little belly seemed to be swelling. Again, she thought about killing herself – but how? It was only a passing thought, nevertheless, it was a thought.

The evening was warm and balmy. She wondered if spending the night at the beach in their little secluded cave would be comforting to her. The sleeping bag was still there and she needed to sleep on it and smell the lingering scent of her Joe.

As she walked toward their hideout on the beach, her mind was completely preoccupied with how to tell her parents that they were going to be grandparents to a child who was an offspring of military personnel. She walked past four or five young Portuguese guys having a good time hanging out around a small beach campfire. They were drinking beer and smoking marijuana. She knew that smell. They whistled at her as she walked by. One started shouting some obscene things at her. She kept her head down and kept walking, pretending not to hear them. She was frightened. This was a very secluded area of the beach. She and Joe never saw anyone else the many times they had met there. Isabel's skirt swung as she tried to walk fast. The breeze lifted her skirt slightly, nearly exposing her panties.

The guys were really drunk and high on the cannabis. They were watching her walk. Then to her horror, they began to follow her. She walked faster and tried to become invisible. It didn't work. They caught up with her and all five of them made a circle around her. They were intoxicated and continued to taunt her and say very crude sexual things to her. The circle started to close in on her. One of them grabbed her around the waist from behind and lifted her up off the sand while two others grabbed her legs, pulled off her pink panties, and spread her knees apart. Each one took his turn with her while she was held suspended in air.

After the last one had his way with her, the other ones just dropped her small, abused body in the sand. One of them kicked sand in her face and called her a filthy name before he ran off to catch up with his buddies. The repulsive group just seemed to disappear as she lay bleeding from her vagina.

Isabel stumbled when she tried to stand. She was much too unsteady to walk. She dragged herself and crawled to the entrance of their hidden cave and fell onto the sleeping bag. The cramps in her abdomen and between her legs seemed to rock her entire body. The pain came in relentless waves. With a sudden gush of bright red blood and an automatic spasm from deep within her, she involuntarily grunted and pushed - expelling the fetus. She lost her baby. Isabel was barely conscious as she lay there in a pool of warm blood. That warm blood contained what should have been her son.

When she woke, the morning light was shining outside the mouth of the little cave. She thought she was too drained to ever move. Thankfully within a few hours she was able to pull herself up and slowly limp a few yards into the lapping waves of the sea. She waded up to her chin and carefully let herself fall backwards. She silently floated back to shore still fully clothed except for her underwear. She let the soothing, salty water wash away the dried blood from between her legs.

Isabel gradually returned to the cave and folded up the blood-soaked sleeping bag. She dragged it outside and stashed it behind some large boulders. She lay down in the soft weeds beside the huge rocks and slept. When she woke, her clothes were dry and the sun was going down. She wondered what her parents must think because all the nights she spent away with Joe, she always showed up early in the morning to help out in the bakery.

Isabel stood up, composed herself as much as possible, finger combed her hair and reluctantly started walking home. She had nowhere else to go.

Her parents rarely spoke to her anymore. When she walked through the back door of their shabby little home, they gasped at the sight of her. She solemnly passed by them and went directly to her room and her cot where she slept for the next several hours. She woke to the smell of the day's bread baking. She washed up, put on fresh clothes and went out to help her parents. They pretended nothing unusual had happened. Both parents glanced her way a few times and knew that something was terribly wrong. Her mother and father were afraid to ask questions because they were fearful of what they might hear.

Two days later, Isabel went to the naval station in an attempt to get word to Joe. She was told that he was on a classified mission and could not receive or send any correspondence. Isabel went back to the bakery. It was all she knew to do; just work day after day after day after day.

Joe had been on assignment for five months when three sailors in dress uniforms along with the chaplain who had officiated her marriage to Joe, stopped by the bakery. The chaplain gave her the news she feared. "There has been an accident," he said. "We are very sorry to inform you that Joe's mission had gone bad during maneuvers." She stood motionless.

The chaplain's lips were quivering as he tried to maintain composure. He continued, "There was a technical malfunction under hazardous conditions, Joe's ship was destroyed during a military exercise. There were, *there were*, (he cleared his throat) no survivors." He reached for Isabel to comfort her, but she pulled away.

Isabel had worried endlessly that something like this had happened. She knew that Joe would have found a way somehow to contact her if he were alive. She stood motionless trying to listen. The words sounded muffled to her.

The naval officers tried to explain to her that there had been an explosion and Joe along with the other men died instantly. One officer, the husky one with a patch over his left eye, said something about practice maneuvers and trying to set some kind of record. The other officer, the tall thin one with the sad eyes, looked down at the ground and said, "The incident is under investigation." The short, red headed officer with the blank eyes, said something about air compression and failed sprinklers and that Isabel was entitled to a copy of the full report if she wished. After a little cough, he lowered his eyes and added, "We prefer to keep the incident quiet from the news media." The chaplain with the caring eyes, told her that she should be proud of Joe as he was a very brave man and gave his life for his country. He continued by saying, "It was an unfortunate accident and no one is sure what lead to the explosion. Is there *anything* I can do for you and your family?" She stared at the ground and slowly just shook her head.

What they didn't tell her was that the bodies of those sailors had been blown to bits. The dead men were identified by dental records being matched to insignias and dog tags.

Isabel was also told that, as his wife, she was entitled to survivor benefits which included a life insurance policy and a small monthly stipend. They presented her with his belongings. She spoke softly as she thanked the gentlemen and excused herself. They quickly turned on their polished heels and left as she took Joe's things to her room and shoved all of it under her cot. She didn't touch anything for several days.

When she was finally strong enough to open the package and box, she found an unopened letter from Joe's father, Stan, with his new address and phone number. Isabel knew she needed to call him. Maybe Stan didn't know that Joe was never coming back. Joe was the only person Stan had in this world and now he would never see him again. Now he had no one.

Isabel wrote to Stan and told him about their tragic loss. Her tears stained every sentence as she put it down on paper. She explained that she and Joe were married only a short time but she thought of him every moment and missed him more than she could put into words.

When Stan read Isabel's letter, he felt sick and nearly threw up. It was as if the air was thick and stale. Breathing was difficult. He staggered to his bed and stayed there until the next day.

His only comfort was in knowing that Joe had known such love of a woman during his brief life. Joe had written all about Isabel in his letters. Stan knew how important she had been to him.

As months went on, letters from Stan and Isabel made their way across the ocean. They were two people who felt a special closeness even though they had never met. Stan was aging and his health was a concern. Isabel was well aware of parents aging as her mother and father were not doing well healthwise. The bakery was turning out less than half of the baked goods they had been used to selling only a few years ago.

Isabel didn't realize how bad things were until her mother became so frail that she stayed in the back room and in her bed most of the time. Isabel's father was shuffling as he walked and had a recurring, hacking cough. One afternoon, he slumped over the counter and slid to the floor. He was dead by the time Isabel got to him. She screamed and two of the town ladies who were in the bakery came around behind the cash register where Isabel's father lay lifeless.

After a quick evaluation, one of the lady's spoke softly to Isabel, "He is dead, my dear."

Isabel knew it too. She went to the back room and found some white bed sheets. The two ladies and Isabel wrapped her father tightly in the sheets and folded the ends in. The three of them carried him to his bed where her mother was sitting on a small wooden chair mumbling something to herself. She barely noticed the women or the body wrapped so tightly in her bed sheets.

Isabel thanked the two ladies who quickly exited out the front door of the bakery.

Isabel called the coroner who would stop in that evening. Burial arrangements were made but only a few people were in attendance. Isabel's mother stayed home.

The bakery was closed indefinitely. Isabel did not want the responsibility of running a bakery by herself. She had a little money each month provided by the US government due to Joe's untimely death. She decided to just spend her days caring for her mother. Because of her past relationship with a sailor from the base and without the bakery, Isabel was pretty much forgotten. The only time anyone really talked to her was someone inquiring when the bakery would be opening again.

As Isabel's mother started noticing that her husband wasn't there anymore, she became more and more confused. She was slipping farther and farther away from reality.

Early one morning Isabel awoke to the smell of smoke. There had been no cooking or baking in weeks so she was alarmed by the heavy odor permeating her room. She got up from her cot and went out into the bakery as quickly as she could.

She found her mother lying on the floor in front of the ovens, which she must have lit because they were red hot. Isabel grabbed her mother at the same time her mother pulled away and went limp. Isabel saw her mother's eyes were open but they were rolled back in her head. Isabel shook her and yelled at her but there was no response. Two more white sheets were needed.

Now, Isabel was totally alone. No family, no friends, no husband, no bakery and no baby. Yes, she often thought of the baby she lost. Oh, how she grieved silently for Joe and for their baby. Her breasts longed for the warm mouth of her infant child. She sometimes would press a pillow to her chest, close her eyes and embrace it as if it were the little one she lost.

There were times when the ladies in Isabel's village would wrap up some clean rags and twist them into a ragdoll for a senile family member to hold.

An elderly woman would cuddle the ragdoll as though it were a child. She would sing, coo and rock her "baby" while losing more and more of her mind, gently slipping into the abyss. Isabel wished sometimes that she had one of those ragdolls to hold and snuggle.

All of Isabel's emotional energy was spent trying to explain to herself why life was so cruel. She grieved. She mourned. She blamed herself for the miscarriage. *If only she had not gone to the beach that day . . .*

Isabel spent the next few months in misery as a recluse in the back rooms of the deteriorating bakery. She read at times and slept at other times.

Occasionally she took a walk to the lonely, deserted place on the path where she and Joe used to meet. She never returned to the beach or to their cave after that terrifying night - the night she tried and tried to forget but never could. Those memories were her enemies. She pushed the sickening images away but they always found a route back to haunt her.

Chapter 9

STRANGE LOVE

A few months after her mother died, Isabel received a letter from Joe's dad, Stan. She was excited to get any mail, let alone correspondence from America. Stan sent his condolences and said he wished that there was some way he could meet Isabel in person. He said he daydreamed that she was coming to Michigan and was planning to visit him. He told her how very lonely he was and wondered if she was lonely, too. He longed to hear stories about Joe.

Isabel, who now had almost no interaction with people, was astounded that he was showing interest in her wellbeing. No one had ever asked her if she was lonely because no one really cared. So much was bottled up inside her. She found herself opening up to Stan. She wrote back to him and tried to explain her circumstances and living arrangements and how alone she was. She didn't tell him of the hollowness that engulfed her, of the days and nights she spent in silent desperation, or how the loneliness was slowly draining the life out of her. She couldn't confide in him and tell him of the times she thought she heard Joe's voice, or his laugh, or thought she felt his warm breath against her hair as she slept.

Stan was relieved and excited when he received a letter back from Isabel. As he read her letter, he could sense great sadness in her words. He read the letter over and over. Her English was passable and her spelling was better than his. He knew what she was saying. He fell asleep with her letter cradled in his lap as though it were a treasure of great value. When he woke from his nap, he knew he had to see her. Stan was not a person who acted on impulse and he had never been on an airplane, but he stepped out of his usual character. The very next day, he purchased two airline tickets for Isabel. Two tickets because she would have to change planes in New York. He would make arrangements to pick her up at Detroit Metropolitan Airport on June 1st. He chose June because he felt the snow and ice would be a thing of the past by then. At least he hoped so.

When Isabel received the tickets, she didn't know whether to laugh or cry, so she did both. The thought of going to America was exciting but also scary to her. She needed to be careful. But spending her days in the backroom of a bakery that was falling down around her was stealing her life. She didn't want to make a decision she would regret . . . to stay or to go.

She'd wait a few days before she answered Stan. Isabel had moved into her parents' room as it was bigger than hers and the bed was more comfortable than her little cot. She tossed and turned unable to sleep, trying to decide whether or not to go to the United States to meet Stan. The sheets were always wadded in a bunch at her feet each morning as she tossed and turned every night.

One particularly gloomy morning she wandered into her old bedroom. She needed to get some light into the little room. When she pushed back the window curtain, she gasped at what she saw. A beautiful small purple flower was somehow stuck to her window. There had been a storm in the night and she guessed a gust of wind had blown the flower up against the glass and the delicate blossom remained caught on the sill. She took a double take and her heart leaped within her when she pushed open the window and retrieved the flower whose beautiful petals were still wet from the recent rain. Isabel took this wonderful little flower as a sign from Joe. A sign that said to go meet his father in America.

Isabel paced around and around in circles trying to hold off until 11:00 AM to call Stan. She wasn't sure what time it was in Michigan but midmorning Azores' time seemed reasonable. Isabel was going to the United States to meet and stay with a man she had never seen. She was finding it hard to breathe.

Stan answered his phone quickly before the second ring. He answered by asking a question, "Hello?" Then Isabel returned his, "Hello?" in a slight accent and also in the form of a question. He knew immediately who was on the other end of the line. "Isabel?" he asked.

"Yes, it's Isabel," she said. "I received the airline tickets. If it is still okay, I will be arriving on June 1st."

"Good, Good," Stan almost shouted into the phone. He could hardly believe his ears. Joe's wife, Stan's daughter-in-law, was coming to meet him. He would soon meet Isabel. "Oh boy! My goodness, you have made me so happy," his voice lowered and cracked a little as he swallowed hard. "Don't worry about anything. I will be at the airport waiting for you," he managed to say. He hung up the phone quickly because his hand was shaking and he didn't want Isabel to hear him crying.

It took Stan a few moments to deal with the news from Isabel - she was really going to visit him. He was shouting from the rooftops when his teenaged neighbor, Tory, stopped to listen. Tory was retrieving his basketball from Stan's yard. The ball had hit the backboard attached to Tory's parents' garage. It bounced sideways and landed near Stan's front steps. Tory heard yelling from inside his neighbor's house and the thought of someone in trouble came to him. Tory knew that Stan was an older gentleman and lived alone, so being a good Eagle Scout, he rapped on the front door to see if things were okay inside.

Stan threw open the door with a huge smile that was not a usual sight on his face. Oh, he was a nice guy all right but quiet and always kept to himself. Tory asked if everything was okay. "Okay? Better than okay! My daughter-in-law is coming for a visit from the Azores Islands," Stan babbled. "She is *really* coming to see me."

"Azores Islands. Is that in Hawaii?" asked Tory.

Stan laughed out loud and Tory laughed out loud, too, just because this dear old guy, whom he barely knew, was laughing so hard. It brought a pleasure to Tory's heart to see someone so . . . so joyous. A bond was quickly forming between the two of them in those few moments as Stan slapped Tory on his back. "Come in, come in, I'll go get us a coke," Stan said as he turned and went into the kitchen. That was the first of many coca-colas they would enjoy drinking together in the days to come.

Tory began going over to his neighbor's just to kill a little time and see what Stan was up to. If there was a nip in the air, they sipped hot chocolate while Tory told Stan about school and about his basketball practice and Stan would tell Tory stories of life on the farm. He would talk about Ruby and Pearl, his two work horses, and how he missed them. He often thought of the days when he walked behind them turning up fresh-smelling earth. Usually it was in the spring after the land had been left dormant for months when the blade of the plow would twist, burying the hard-top soil while forcing the damp, fertile ground to the top. Planting would soon follow. Tory had never been on a farm, but he loved to hear and visualize the scene as Stan told stories.

The day finally arrived when Isabel was to fly into Metro Airport. Stan asked Tory if he wanted to ride along with him. The truth was really that Stan was a little shaky about how to get to the airport and what to do once he got there. The highways were well-marked, but his eyesight was never very good. Tory, on the other hand, was young. He was strong, athletic and had great eyesight. He'd be able to help carry Isabel's luggage.

So, the two buddies, one old and one young, unstuck Stan's deteriorating garage door which hadn't been opened in weeks. The door creaked and moaned and groaned and shook a little, but it finally gave in and let loose to allow Stan and Tory inside. They sort of dusted the old car off with a couple of rags that were hanging on a nail. Stan always named his cars – this one was the Brown Bomber. Stan wouldn't let Tory drive. He just wasn't ready to let go of his ability to handle his Brown Bomber. It surprised them when that darn car started up on the second try. Stan drove as Tory had a death grip on the passenger's side door handle. He thought if Stan drove any slower, they could be all day just getting to the airport. They did make it on time. When Isabel came through the gates, Tory was carrying a bouquet of daisies with long stems, Stan was holding up an 8 1/2 X 11 card "ISABEL." She didn't know how she would recognize Stan or how to find him . . . well, that was no problem.

As they reached each other, Tory shyly grinned and handed her the flowers, while Stan stood there fumbling around with the sign not knowing whether to throw it away or keep it. There were no hugs. Stan sure wasn't used to hugs and since Joe's death, Isabel had not been hugged by anyone. There were no thoughts of hugging each other. The first few moments were a little awkward, even though there were no expectations on either side.

Tory was surprised when he saw Isabel. She looked younger than he expected. She was so small. Her dark brown eyes were the only large thing about her and they had a sadness about them. Stan finally found his voice and asked where they should go to get her luggage. "Oh," she said, "this is my luggage," and she pointed to a small cloth carry-on tote bag. "This is all I brought." Truthfully, she only had a few things to bring.

Isabel was wearing her best dress which was pale pink with a matching short jacket. The color enhanced the qualities of her dark skin. She looked so pretty to Tory and Stan. Tory grabbed the so-called suitcase while Stan led her to the car by holding her elbow with one hand and continuing to hold the "IS-ABEL" sign with the other. Isabel held the bouquet of daisies and her little clutch purse that held lip gloss, comb, a handkerchief and a couple American dollars. Isabel sat in the backseat. She hadn't ridden in very many automobiles and was trying to understand who all the cars belonged to that were parked in the airline parking lots. Countless numbers of vehicles were also on the highway. *Where were all these people going?* she wondered. She had seen hundreds of people during the last twenty-four hours but not many resembled her.

Isabel's flawless, soft skin looked tanned. Her hair was so black that it glistened when it caught the sun. Her eyes were the color of rich chocolate. She looked different in a pleasing way. Isabel stood five feet tall and wore a size zero in store-bought clothes. Her hands were the only thing that gave away the hard work she had done since she was eight or nine years old. Scraping and washing pan after pan, cookie sheets and muffin tins all in steaming hot water had taken a toll on her delicate hands. Hot ovens had burned her fingers and scrubbing the floor at the end of each day had left her hands raw at times.

Talking was not easy for her even though she could read and write in two languages. She had spent long lonely hours reading the newspapers that were always thrown at the bakery door. It was surprising that she was up on world events, because she lived like a recluse. Her parents had taken her out of school when she was thirteen. They felt she knew everything she needed to know to run the bakery - if and when they couldn't.

Stan, Tory and Isabel were a unique threesome. Stan was aging, stooped and looked older than he was. His hands were disfigured due to arthritis and years of tending crops and looking after his farm. Next to the two of them, Tory looked tall and muscular. He had a mop of golden-brown hair and gorgeous blue-gray eyes, enhanced by thick blonde eyelashes and heavy eyebrows. When he smiled, deep dimples formed in his cheeks.

The three headed for the small bungalow where Stan lived alone. There wasn't much conversation during the ride. Isabel was mesmerized by the amount of traffic, the bridges, overpasses and the high-rise buildings that seemed to line the main road.

Stan didn't know what to say or how to start up a conversation. Tory was still trying to figure out where the Azores Islands were and who exactly this quiet unfamiliar girl was in the backseat. He noticed that her eyes were fixed on what was going on outside of the car as they journeyed toward Flint.

Tory was used to women wearing makeup. Almost all of them he was familiar with wore at least lipstick and most wore mascara. He knew a few girls who wore a lot of makeup almost as a disguise to hide on the outside who they were inside. But here was this young woman, named Isabel, who was without any kind of "mask." He loved seeing her real untouched face, not hiding who she was or trying to look like something she wasn't.

As Stan pulled the old Brown Bomber into his driveway, Isabel was trying to grasp the idea that Stan lived in a three-bedroom home all alone. She didn't know what to expect and was pleased at how pleasant the house looked when she saw it for the first time. The yard was small but nice. She allowed herself a deep breath and could smell that the lush green grass had been freshly cut. Thick, tall shrubs lined the property between Stan's home and Tory's. There was an opening through the bushes where Tory had worn a path from his house to Stan's.

Tory lived in the brick two-story Colonial next door with his parents. He had two older brothers who were married. One lived in New Mexico and one in California. For the most part, Tory felt like an only child. He was the "baby" but wasn't really babied. His parents were hard-working people who loved their jobs. Tory knew that he was loved also, even though his mom and dad never said, "I love you." He always felt it and the security that went with it.

Isabel thought Tory's home looked like a bed and breakfast she had seen in a travel magazine. She never expected to see such a lovely place in her lifetime with its stone work and red shutters. A curved slate walkway led to the front door.

Tory noticed Isabel staring at his home as he carried her bag to Stan's front porch. He was proud of the house he lived in, although for some reason at this moment when Isabel took special notice of it, he was embarrassed by the richness of its design.

Tory turned and asked Stan which room Isabel would be staying in as he was setting her bag down. Stan said to let her take her pick. Stan reached deep into his front pants pocket and found a key. He opened the front door and stood back allowing Isabel to enter first.

As she stepped into Stan's living room onto beige carpeting, her eyes swept the room. A tan sofa, a faded rose-colored platform rocker and a small, maple coffee table were in the living room along with two lamps and a television set. The TV set had about a twelve-inch screen and 'rabbit ears' antennas. No drapes or curtains, only wide dusty Venetian blinds hung at the windows for privacy. The kitchen was to the left of the living room. There was a small bay window and in front of the window was a round table with three chairs upholstered in red Naugahyde. The view from the window was the small front yard and the paved street. A few cupboards, stove, refrigerator and sink with some counterspace completed the little kitchen. Through the kitchen was the door that led to the basement. Isabel was expecting the basement to be musty and damp, but it wasn't. There was a small, bare window at the top of each of the four cement-block walls. A wash tub, a washing machine and a few storage bins lined one wall. The basement, while neat and tidy, was plain with a poured cement floor. Clotheslines were draped across the ceiling to hang wet garments to dry. Clothespins clung loosely to the lines awaiting the next wash day.

Back up the stairs returning to the main floor were three small bedrooms behind the living room. The first one on the left was yellow and white with a twin bed, night stand, a small dresser and a tiny closet. The lone window provided a soft breeze that Isabel could feel from across the room. The next room was the bathroom. There was a tub but no shower. The thought of relaxing in a warm tub of water crossed Isabel's mind. Next were two more bedrooms. Stan slept in the biggest room which was at the very back of the house. It was a dark room and it didn't help that Stan never opened the blinds. The last room she saw was used as a 'catch all.' In that room there was a dusty ancient desk collecting papers, books and unopened mail. In the corner of the room were boxes of stuff that no longer held anything of importance.

Isabel quickly chose the yellow and white room with its view of the backyard, driveway and an old, whitewashed one-car garage. The closet in the yellow room was the smallest in the house but her belongings couldn't begin to fill it.

Stan asked her if she would like to rest a bit before dinner. "Oh yes," she said quietly. "I would like that very much."

Alone in her little room she felt a rush of happiness. She couldn't remember the last time she felt such contentment. That wonderful feeling washed over her and she let out the big breath she had been unconsciously holding in. She slipped off her shoes and stretched out on the little Jenny Lind bed. She stared up at the ceiling and tried to sort out the day and what she was feeling here with Joe's dad. She was in a foreign country with people she didn't know. Much to her surprise, she felt comfortable. She closed her eyes and napped feeling safe.

After she had rested and was a bit refreshed, she left her little yellow room. She smelled something cooking. She went into the kitchen where Stan was preparing a dinner of hamburgers, potato chips and iced tea with lemon slices. Tory left to have dinner with his mom and dad even though he was thinking those hamburgers were smelling good. Isabel felt a tenderness towards Stan as he stood cooking a meal for her. Together they sat at the table in front of the bay window on the red kitchen chairs and ate chips and the juicy burgers with mustard, ketchup, pickles and onions.

Isabel and Stan joined forces and together cleaned up the kitchen. They stayed up for hours that first night. Stan was hanging on every word Isabel said. She told him everything. Well, *almost* everything. Her short courtship with Joe, their marriage and him being shipped out. Isabel cried as she told Stan about the naval officials coming to the bakery and telling her of Joe's accident. She even told Stan about how her parents had barely spoken to her for several months. However, she *didn't* tell him about her pregnancy or the rape or about losing Joe's baby. Those were still private, painful secrets that she never wanted to think about — *let alone talk about.*

The fondness between Stan and Isabel was something neither had expected. It was developing so quickly. Two lonely people were no longer lonely. As the days passed, the two of them grew closer and closer. The more they got to know one another, the more Isabel realized how important sports were to Stan. She soon started to join him in front of the TV set when the Tigers played baseball. She learned to cheer for their team and boo the umps. They shared reading the daily paper, they often fixed meals together, ate together and went about household duties together. They were starting to finish each other's sentences. Stan secretly began to think of her like the daughter he never had and she began to think of him like the loving father hers should have been . . . but wasn't.

Chapter 10

LOVE GROWS

Stan was quickly getting used to having Isabel around. As the weeks passed, Stan and Isabel were growing to depend on one another. After she had been living there for about six weeks, Stan shyly asked her, "Could you possibly, I mean, would you consider staying here? Um, maybe you could think about, you know, building a life in America. I hope I'm not being forward or pushy. I guess I sound like a goofy old man. Well, please just think about it. I'm sorry if I offended you."

Isabel was painfully aware that she didn't have anything to go back to. The Azores Islands were fading in her memories and besides she was loving America. She was starting to enjoy living again. She felt safe and loved. Financially Isabel was okay because of her small income from the Navy. Stan didn't owe anyone anything. There weren't a lot of expenses.

She only had to think a day or so about Stan's invitation to stay with him when she took his gnarled old hands in hers and looked straight into his eyes and said, "Of course, I'll stay in America. Isn't that what a daughter-in-law should do?" She gave him a smile that melted his frail heart. Her teeth were straight and white, her lips were soft and full, her smile was always sincere.

Tory stopped by almost every day and gave them a play-by-play accounting of his high school experiences. Since neither Stan nor Isabel had attended high school, they were always delighted to be his audience. Even though Tory's parents usually weren't home, he had listeners who were attentive when he went next door.

Stan had missed high school because he started working on the family farm when he was about nine or ten. As a youngster on his parents' farm he would open the door of the chicken coop at dawn, rousting the clucking hens outside so he could get inside to gather their eggs. The eggs were often still warm from the mother hen's body that had been protecting them. Stan didn't mind the smell of the chicken coop and the warm eggs felt good to his cold hands as he carefully picked each one from its comfortable little nest made of straw and feathers. He would then go back to the house taking the eggs to the kitchen. By the time he reached the back step he could smell bacon grease sizzling in an iron skillet. His mom would be at the stove, her hair tied back with a string, waiting for the eggs. She was short and stout and wore an apron all day every day. She would crack each egg with one hand and plop it into the crackling grease. Stan would eat his fried egg on top of a warm piece of homemade bread that had been smeared with freshly-churned butter. He ate every delicious bite while he headed out to the barn to help with whatever had to be done. As a child, he often wished he could taste the white sliced bread in the grocery store that came in a bag. He assumed that it must taste really good 'cause it cost money. He thought that store-bought bread had to be a lot better than the home-made stuff he had to eat. *Today* he would give just about anything to have a hunk of that bread his mom used to fix for him.

Isabel's first memories were that of helping her parents in the bakery - not of school, teachers, friends, crayons or recess. There had been little time for schooling for Stan or Isabel which made Tory's reenactments of his day at high school most interesting and entertaining. Tory's dad was a successful salesman and traveled about twenty days out of each month. Mostly he sold shipping pallets to automobile companies. Tory's mom was a registered nurse and assisted in short-stay surgery at the local hospital. She worked rotating hours and picked up extra shifts when one of the other nurses needed a day off. She was a very good nurse and loved her job which meant she wasn't home much either. Not a problem, Tory always had a welcoming audience with Stan and Isabel.

Tory would imitate his coach bouncing a basketball and barking at his players. Then he would pretend to be holding the basketball and skip, and jump, and toss in a perfect basket in an invisible hoop in Stan's living room.

Tory would mimic how the 'starters' on the team would walk around all puffed up with their chests stuck out and their noses in the air all the while a group of adoring girls followed them down the halls. Sometimes Tory would be taking big steps across Stan's cramped living room. He would crouch and pretend to bounce a basketball and jump up again showing Stan and Isabel how he tipped in a basket for two points. Stan and Isabel would clap and Tory would take a little bow. Sometimes he pretended to miss a layup and would grimace and put his hands in front of his face to cover the embarrassment of missing an easy shot. Stan and Isabel would try to console him with words of encouragement.

The three of them played poker for pennies almost every night. Stan could hold his own, winning more coins than he lost. There were even times when Isabel and Tory looked the other way to allow Stan to cheat a little.

Tory had become closer to Stan and Isabel than to his own parents. They knew his schedule, his friends' names, his likes, his dislikes, and his thoughts on many subjects. They were an unlikely threesome, nonetheless, they looked forward to seeing one another almost daily to share stories and play cards or dominoes.

Time passed so fast that they couldn't believe Tory would be graduating from high school soon. He was fortunate to be able to attend college in the fall. He wanted to major in Law Enforcement and applied to Ferris Institute in Big Rapids when life took terrible turn.

Stan was sitting in his wicker rocker on the front porch drinking a cup of lukewarm coffee and struggling with a crossword puzzle that was in the morning paper. He had been thinking about starting up the Brown Bomber. His car had been sitting silent for quite a while in the garage. That garage had also become home to a family of mice and an orphaned raccoon. He was trying to remember where he had put the car keys.

Just then a yellow taxi cab pulled up in front of the house. Isabel had been shopping and was collecting herself and her purchases while she exited the cab. The taxi driver waved at Stan and pulled away from the curb as Isabel was smiling and walking towards Stan's porch. Suddenly three young teenaged boys appeared on the sidewalk in front of her. They started ogling her and whistling. They were puckering their lips and making smacking sounds in the air as if they were kissing her. Stan shouted at them and tried to stand but the thugs laughed at him and called him an asshole. Stan was hollering, yelling and trying to get to them, when he lost his balance, and fell down the porch steps.

Isabel was losing control of her faculties. She had dropped her packages and was sliding to the ground while the hoodlums, who wreaked of alcohol, taunted her and told her to bend over so they could get a good look at her backside. They started to circle her.

Isabel crumpled down into a ball on the sidewalk crying uncontrollably - all the time shaking and talking to herself in sounds that came from somewhere deep within her soul. Her mind was suddenly thrust back to the brutal attack on the beach in the Azores when she was raped and discarded like garbage. She wailed as if she was wounded when she remembered losing the baby that had been growing inside of her – Joe's baby. Unthinkable memories she had been suppressing for a very long time, flooded her like a tsunami.

Tory, who was in his home next door at the dining room table struggling with his Geometry homework, heard the loud voices and immediately went out his front door just in time to see one of the young thugs run over and kick Stan in the stomach. Tory panicked when he saw the other two put themselves in front of Isabel as she lay on the sidewalk whimpering and whispering under her breath in Portuguese. Her eyes were glazed over. She had mentally left the scene.

Tory disregarded his usual good judgment and went running towards the violence. He grabbed the teenaged rebel closest to him and kneed him in the groin. He grabbed the second one and slugged him so hard he broke his nose. Blood was squirting everywhere. Just as Tory turned to get the one who had kicked Stan, the drunken kid pulled out a knife. When Tory lunged himself onto the guy, the knife penetrated Tory's left thigh. The knife was twisted hard into his thigh until Tory became completely helpless. The thug then stomped on Tory's leg until he heard bone crunching.

Stan was on the ground suffering and moaning, Tory was writhing in excruciating pain, and Isabel was hysterical and lying in a fetal position on the sidewalk babbling incoherently in her native tongue. The young criminal grabbed up his buddies and the three disappeared around the nearest corner.

Stan heroically managed to drag himself into the house and phone for help.

Stan, Isabel and Tory were taken to the hospital. Tory's parents were summoned. They didn't know what to expect to see or hear when they arrived. They thought possibly a sport's injury . . . maybe torn ACL.

The trauma surgeon, Dr. Grant, entered the room wearing a starched-white shirt, camel-colored corduroy blazer, perfectly pressed brown trousers, and leather loafers. He hadn't taken time to change from his street clothes into his scrubs before he started by telling them that Tory was indeed a hero. . . . but that the femur in his left leg needed to be operated on immediately. Dr. Grant and assisting staff would try to put the leg back together using screws and pins in the damaged thigh. He explained that the procedure works better for some than for others.

Tory's parents were devastated when they heard the whole awful story and learned that their handsome son may always walk with a limp. They took the news harder than Tory. His father paced back and forth and shouted, "Who did this? Who are these good for nothing bums? I will see that they are going to be put away for a very, very long time. And I mean a very long time. Let me get my hands on them!" He made a fist and pounded it into palm of his other hand.

Tory's mother just sat crying, blowing her nose, and repeatedly saying, "I just can't believe this, I just can't believe it. My beautiful son. I just can't believe it."

Tory was not sorry for jumping into a disastrous situation to help Stan and Isabel. He felt that sometimes you just have to do what you have to do. He had no regrets. He would have gone up against an army for Stan and Isabel. His only regret was that he hadn't caused more physical damage to the guys who hurt him. He felt sick when he found out they had disappeared without a trace.

Stan and Isabel were kept at the hospital for a few hours and then sent home. The police officer who had been assigned to the case drove them so he could ask more questions and get more information about the three boys who had attacked them. The officer had a husky build and a scruffy beard. He was in his 50s and had seen his share of violence. His twenty-five years on the force had hardened him to the evilness of his world. He was kind and respectful to Stan and Isabel. He helped them into their house and then returned to his cruiser. He had asked them all the right questions while chewing on the filter tip of an unlit cigarette. He quit smoking two years ago but still just felt better with a cigarette between his lips.

The officer didn't have the heart to tell them that there wasn't a chance in hell that the three punks who hurt them would be apprehended. The city had numerous kids who fit the descriptions he had been given. *'What could he do?'* He had long ago given up looking for the proverbial needle in the haystack.

The next morning, Stan and Isabel went out to the old shabby garage, got into the Brown Bomber and chugged to the hospital in time to be there when Tory woke from surgery. When they were allowed to see him, Tory's pleasant face was now pale and expressionless. The surgery had gone well. Pins, screws and years of experience were all the trauma surgeon needed to put the badly injured femur back together. He told Tory's mom and dad and Stan and Isabel that recovery would take months and that Tory might always walk with some pain and may need the help of a cane. But at least they were able to save Tory's leg.

After a few days recovering in the hospital trauma unit, Tory was transported by ambulance to a skilled nursing facility. He was confined to a wheelchair unable to put any weight on his surgical leg for three months. He was taken to the physical therapy wing twice a day every day. Since he was so young and in good physical condition, he caught on very fast as to what to do. Transferring to and from the bed, using the restroom and showering by sitting on a bench with his leg propped up on a waste basket soon became routine. Young female aides who attended him didn't mind a bit when he pushed his "help needed" button. Anne was his favorite. She was a tall blue-eyed blonde who didn't know how attractive she was. She had always been big for her age and felt gawky and unsophisticated. Anne spent extra time with Tory. Her coffee breaks were often spent sitting in his little private room telling him about her horse named JoJo and the barrel races she and JoJo competed in at the County fair. She showed him pictures of herself riding on the spotted horse nearly falling as they rounded the barrels with her leaning into the turn.

Tory, being raised in town, had never even ridden a horse and was fascinated and enjoyed hearing her talk with such enthusiasm about an animal. He loved hearing her talk about anything for that matter. She was his connection to what was going on in the outside world.

His parents visited every day but they didn't always look at his leg which was held stationary in a removable brace. They were probably too afraid of what they might see. Tory was often relieved when they left so that Anne could talk privately to him. She was confiding more and more in him and he enjoyed it. He loved Anne … but not in a romantic way. She had become his best friend.

A few days before he was released from the nursing center, Anne stepped into his room, closed the door behind her and sat in the chair nearest his bed. She looked sad. Her mascara was smeared, and Tory knew she had been crying. "What's wrong?" he asked. He was truly concerned about her.

Anne put her hands over her face and without looking at him, she said, "I missed my period for the last three months." Tory had to take a few minutes to compute what she was saying. He didn't even know she had a serious boy-friend. "Who have you been seeing?" he asked.

Through trembling lips, she explained, "A friend fixed me up with this guy, and we've been seeing each other for the last few months. One night at a "grasser", you know . . . a party held in a field, we had too much to drink and ended up in the bed of his pickup truck until daylight. We made love in a bit of a drunken haze. I hardly remember it."

Tory was trying to think of something to say. "What are you going to do?" he finally asked.

"I don't know yet," she sobbed.

"Do you want to marry this guy?" he asked.

"No," she wailed. "He got engaged to some girl in Ohio." Tory tried to reach for her hand. She stood up out of his reach ashamed and embarrassed. She awkwardly left his room and closed the door behind her.

Tory was soon to be released from the center and would receive further physical therapy at home. He still saw Anne almost every day. She was always kind and helpful but was now somewhat distant when they spoke.

Meanwhile, Stan and Isabel were very busy hammering together a ramp to push Tory and his wheelchair in and out of Stan's house.

Chapter 11

WHERE IS LOVE

*T*ory was determined to walk and even run again. He knew it was up to him to work hard at getting strong. He was a fighter and his efforts were paying off. He was allowed out of his wheelchair by using crutches to steady himself as he hopped on his right leg without putting any weight on the injured leg. He was showing miraculous improvement. His recovery surprised everyone, including his trauma surgeon. Tory wasn't raised in a church-going family, even so, in his private moments he thanked God for his recovery.

Anne came into Tory's room as he was packing up his belongings getting ready to go home. She had punched out on the time clock looking pale and feeling depressed. She said, "I plan to have my baby without any attempt at letting the baby's father know that I'm carrying his child. I will have to quit the evening classes I'm taking to become a physical therapist. I want to be a good mom."

She watched Tory pack his suitcase and thought about how much she would miss him. It wasn't permitted to contact patients once they left the facility. She couldn't imagine not being able to see him every day. He had been her trusted friend and the only person who knew her secret. Anne sat down in the chair next to the window. Her eyes were rimmed with dark circles. She looked like she hadn't slept at all last night.

"How are you doing?" Tory asked.

"Not great," she responded without looking at him. "I'm going to have to tell my parents that they are going to have a grandchild."

"I wish I could be with you when you tell them," he said searching the distressed look on her face.

"Oh no, you don't. I don't know what my parents will say or do when they find out," she said in a very low soft voice as she slowly shook her head from side to side.

"When do you plan to tell them?" he asked.

"Tonight, when I get home. I've got to tell them. I'm tortured with this secret," she said trying not to cry.

Anne looked at Tory with the saddest eyes he had ever seen. He was worried about her. They had become the closest of friends throughout his and her troubled darkest days. He would truly miss Anne. During his time as her patient, he shared things with her that he had never shared with anyone. Just things like his favorite movies, favorite books, plans for life and his relationship with his parents. He told Anne things he hadn't even told his loyal confidants, Stan and Isabel.

Anne left the room slowly and quietly closed the door behind her. Tory was positive that he would continue to see her after he went home. He knew he couldn't ask for her phone number because she could be fired for breaking the rules by having a relationship with a patient. However, he knew her last name and had already looked up her home phone number and he planned to use that number.

When Anne arrived home that evening, her mother was in the kitchen leaning over the ironing board carefully pressing her dad's white shirt. Steam was rising from the iron as she took particular care to get the collar just right. She was preoccupied with her own personal perfectionism when Anne entered the room.

"Mom, I need to talk to you," she said in a soft but determined voice. Her mom shook the shirt out and was putting it on a hanger. She didn't want to be bothered right now with whatever her daughter wanted to talk about.

Her mother turned slightly and was now looking at her. "Mom, I've done something terrible," Anne said as she started to tremble. She starting to cry. "I'm, I'm pregnant," she sobbed. "I'm so embarrassed," she moaned. "Oh, Mom, I'm so ashamed of myself." She was trying to wipe her eyes and nose with the sleeve of the new beige sweater she was wearing.

Her mother steadied herself against the ironing board. She was trying to understand the words her daughter had just dropped on her. She stood still…

rolling everything around in her head. She never thought about Anne being sexually active. *Who, what, when, and where?* Anne was weeping and trembling as she went to her mother with her arms open for some kind of comfort. Her mother raised her arms too, though in anger. She slapped Anne across the face as hard as she could, leaving a bright red hand-mark on her cheek.

"You little bitch. What have you done?" she screamed as she left the kitchen and went into her bedroom, slamming the door leaving Anne looking at an iron that was standing erect, spouting steam on the empty ironing board ready for the next garment.

She could hear her mother crying and it sounded like she was throwing things. She was muttering under her breath, *"What will our neighbors say? Will my sewing circle ladies gossip about us? What about our pastor and what will the church congregation think? I will never be able to show my face in public again with everyone pointing fingers at me."*

It was getting dark outside when Anne heard her father come home from his office at the bank. He was hungry and expected to walk into the house to see his wife setting the table with her favorite dishes on her matching placemats getting ready for their dinner. She would be busy with whatever was cooking on the stove and without really seeing him would say in a sing-song voice, *"It's almost ready."* Except not this night. There was an eerie silence in his home. Nothing was cooking on the stove. The ironing board and laundry were occupying the kitchen. Something was wrong tonight. He felt a tightness in his chest. *What was going on?*

Anne heard her father cautiously rap on his own bedroom door before he opened it. He found his wife wilted and disheveled. "What the hell is going on?" he demanded, as he stared in near disbelief at the woman he had been married to for over twenty years.

He had never seen her looking such a mess. She forced herself to sit up and shouted at him, "Your daughter is a pregnant bitch." Her face looked twisted and out of shape when she looked up at him.

Anne's dad felt like he just entered the outer limits of the Twilight Zone. "What did you say?" he asked. He was dumbfounded.

"It's true. She's a fornicator and she'll rot in hell," she shrieked and fell back down on their bed. He sat down on the side of the bed, even though his wife never allowed him to sit on the side of the bed because she thought it would wear down the mattress edges.

"Please tell me what you are talking about," he stammered.

"Anne got herself in a family way. I don't know who the father is and I don't care who he is. She will have to leave our home. She can't live here. I will not have that . . . that girl ruin our reputation," she spat out.

He stood. He usually stood straight with his shoulders back and walked with a self-assured gait. But now as he went out into the living room to be alone, he was stooped over, with his head down and was heavy-footed as he walked. *Anne pregnant?* This was something he could hardly believe. His wonderful little girl was pregnant. *How can this be?* He loosened his tie as he sat down in his favorite over-stuffed chair looking for anything familiar to give him some feeling of normalcy. This couldn't be happening. He did not have any dinner that evening and he didn't see Anne or his wife the rest of the night. He spent the entire time alone in their living room sitting in his chair staring at the floor trying to make sense of what his wife had just told him.

In the morning he called his office, and for the first time in ten years, he asked his secretary to cancel his appointments for the day - not offering any explanation to the surprise in her voice.

As daylight started to fill the house, Anne was the first to leave her room and join him in the living room. She couldn't help noticing the defeated look of her father. She was his only child and although he rarely expressed his feelings for her, he loved her deeply. He had been up all-night thinking about what to do. Anne looked terrible. He instinctively looked at her abdomen trying to visualize a baby inside her and trying not to visualize how it got there.

Anne was barefoot and wearing her pink flannel pajamas that had panda bears on the collar and cuffs. She flopped down on the sofa and curled her feet under her. She was miserable but at least now her secret was out and with that came some sense of relief. Her plan was to live at home and after she delivered, she would set up a nursery in one half of her bedroom.

"Did Mom tell you about me?" she asked.

"Yes, she did." Her dad was not really looking at her. "Do you love your boyfriend?" he asked, still not looking at her.

Not looking at him, she stared at the floor and said, "No, no, I don't have a boyfriend. He was just someone I hardly knew. I'm not sure why I did what I did. I can't explain it. We were at a party having fun. We started kissing and fooling around and the next thing I know, I'm pregnant." Now she was looking at him, "*Oh Daddy*, I'm so sorry. I won't ask you and mom for anything I promise. I'll take all the responsibility in caring for it."

"Where do you plan to live?" he asked. Now he was looking at her.

"What do you mean?" she asked. She was suddenly confused and frightened. Now she was looking at him. "I'll just stay here with you and mom," she answered, as she searched the troubled look on his face.

"Well, your mother doesn't want you here anymore." he said in a flat voice.

"What are you saying? Where will I go?" she asked as fear was getting a grip on her.

"You should have thought about that when you were, how did you put it, *fooling around*," he said. Now he was looking out the window at his well-manicured yard. He couldn't force himself to look at Anne. His beautiful daughter was disgusting to him. She suddenly seemed dirty. She was almost like a stranger to him.

Anne quietly left the room and went to the kitchen, grabbed a box of peanut butter crackers and escaped to her room. The next morning she showered quickly trying to put herself together enough to get to work. As she started out the front door, her mother yelled out in a strange hoarse voice, "You have one week to find someplace else to live."

Anne quietly closed the front door behind her and drove to work lost in a trance. She was only half-conscious and didn't even know how she arrived at work. She was a little early. Now she had to say goodbye to Tory.

Isabel and Stan were in his room waiting for him to be released. Tory's parents signed the official paperwork and left. They appreciated their neighbors for helping get their son home as they had demands waiting for them at work. Taking time off right now was not only inconvenient but nearly impossible.

Isabel and Stan were resolute in their decision to watch over Tory as he healed and regained all of his strength. To them, it was a gift to care for him... a gift of purpose. They had a purpose in life now, not to mention that they owed him so much for coming to their rescue that horrible afternoon when they were assaulted.

When Anne came into the room, Isabel and Stan excused themselves and went to get a cup of coffee, giving Anne and Tory time to say their goodbyes. Anne closed the door after them so she could speak privately to Tory. She still had the red mark on her cheek where her mother had slapped her. Anne told

Tory all that happened when her parents found out she was pregnant. She said hopelessly, "I'm completely at a loss as to where I will go to live and what I'll do when the baby's born. I am so terribly sorry for how I got this way and wished over and over I could take back the night spent in the bed of a pick-up truck."

Anne considered an abortion and concluded that was not an option. She just could not add to the overwhelming guilt that was now her constant companion by making it worse. She could not destroy the life growing inside of her.

A nurse entered Tory's room and gave him discharge instructions. Anne went to punch in at the time clock and started her workday like a zombie.

All went well with Tory getting home even though he was worried about Anne and her dilemma. Isabel and Stan didn't have to help him very much. He was strong and independent. He was waiting for his parents to come home that night because he had a big favor to ask them. They had plenty of room in their home for Anne. He had a plan. During dinner of chicken noodle soup and grilled cheese sandwiches, he explained Anne's predicament and came right to the point, "I'm asking if she could stay with us temporarily."

His parents looked at each other and with their eyes agreed this was not a good plan. His mom explained, "It just isn't appropriate to have a single, pregnant girl come live in our home with both of your parents away most of the time. Tory, we think the world of Anne." Unfortunately, the answer was "No". It just was not an acceptable living arrangement. Tory felt defeated.

The next morning after Tory's parents left for work, Isabel knocked on his front door. She brought Tory a homemade blueberry muffin, like the ones she used to bake back home in the Azores. She poured him a glass of cold milk and the two of them sat at the table while Tory unloaded the nightmare Anne was living.

Isabel's mind immediately went back to herself when she was pregnant with Joe's baby and didn't know what to do with nowhere to turn. Isabel was quiet for a very long time, just sitting watching Tory enjoy eating his still warm muffin.

He looked up after the last crumb disappeared and said, "Isabel, Anne has no place to live. My parents won't let her come here. I don't care how it looks to other people. My friends would understand, I know they would. Everyone loves Anne."

Isabel's heart was racing. *Would Stan agree to having Anne stay with them for a few months, she wondered.* She knew that Stan thought highly of the lovely girl who had gone out of her way to help them and Tory. Isabel stood up and asked, "Will you be okay if I leave you by yourself for a while?"

He said, "Sure, my buddy, Hank, from school is coming over to watch a war movie on TV. I'll be just fine. I don't need a thing. I'll phone you if that changes." He flashed her one of his movie-star smiles.

She hurried to tell Stan about Anne being forced out of her parents' home with no place to live. "Yes, Anne made a mistake, but who of us can throw the first stone? We have all messed up somewhere, haven't we?" she asked. "Is there any way you and I can help her for a little while?"

Stan listened to Isabel and felt sympathy and sadness. His own past held rough times and he did feel a special connection to Anne. He was concerned that his extra bedroom was presently being used as a storage closet. Where would we put her? Isabel assured him that she could clean up that spare room enough for a temporary living place for Anne. Tory was stunned when Isabel called and told him they wanted to offer Stan's extra room to Anne until she could make other arrangements.

Anne would be getting out of work at 4:00 PM. Tory, Isabel and Stan were waiting in the parking lot in the Brown Bomber. Anne clocked out of work and walked to her car. It startled her when Tory called out to her. She quickly went over to them. He asked her to get into Stan's car for a minute. She was confused. She couldn't have guessed why they were there or what they were about to say.

Isabel did the talking - woman to woman. She told Anne of a time when she found herself in such despair with no one to help her and no place to turn. She explained that she and Stan would love to have her stay with them until she could make better arrangements. Anne could hardly believe what she just heard.

"Oh, Isabel, thank you," Anne sobbed. "When? When can I come?"

Isabel was sensing a joy she hadn't felt since before Joe died. She was reaching out to someone who was in despair and it felt good. "Give me a day or two to set up your room. How about Saturday?"

Anne's parents didn't care where she went as long as she wasn't with them. They let her take her car and belongings and bid her good riddance.

There is an old saying *"One man's trash is another man's treasure."* Anne was trash to her parents . . . but a treasure to Isabel and Stan.

Chapter 12

UNCONDITIONAL LOVE

*A*nne moved what few things she owned into Stan's little house. She wasn't a clothes horse and only had a few outfits because she wore a uniform to work every day. She just had to make three trips from her car to her room before everything was in. Isabel had cleaned the room, washed the off-white walls and put a twin sized bed and dresser where an old desk and storage boxes used to be. The bedspread and curtain were of a matching colorful abstract floral pattern that brightened what used to be a dark dreary mess. The flowers were purple, blue and fuchsia. Various colors of green leaves overlapped each other and the flowers. The fluffy throw rug that covered two thirds of the floor was lime green.

The house was feeling somewhat cramped and crowded, nevertheless, to Isabel and Stan it was more than all right. Anne hadn't expected such a lovely room and such a warm welcome. She would soon start to feel the fluttering of her baby's movement inside her. She kept working at the health facility trying to save enough money to pay for the hospital's delivery charges when the time came. She found that she was becoming more tired than usual, thankfully she had a pretty little room to come home to each night and people who cared about her.

Isabel gladly evolved into the role of cook, housekeeper and Stan's overseer. She loved Anne living with them and soon there would be a baby. A baby! No one knew about the nights when Isabel was haunted by dreams of a baby crying. She would try to follow the sound of the cries; except she always woke up in a sweat before she ever found the baby.

Stan was aging and was so grateful not to be alone. Now he had two nurse-maids, Isabel and Anne, who were ready to watch over him day and night.

Tory's recovery surprised everyone. His injured leg healed completely. No one expected him to do so well. When his surgeon mentioned that he may never walk without a cane, he said, "I'll prove you wrong, Doc." And he did. He was healthy of body and mind. There was no reasonable explanation . . . no limp, no cane. He was as strong and fit as anyone his age and could swagger better than most. He was left with a three-inch scar on his upper thigh and a five-inch scar going down across his knee; other than that he was unscathed. He was busy finishing up his high school degree by way of a home-schooling program. When he had extra time, he could always be found in Stan's time-worn garage tinkering with the Brown Bomber. He loved working on that old car and Stan took pride in the fact that a young guy like Tory would take such an interest in something of his. Tory would wash and shine that ancient auto. It almost seemed as if you could hear the old Brown Bomber sighing as Tory polished its hood with a soft cloth.

Stan allowed Tory to "borrow" the Brown Bomber on occasion. Tory often would pick up a couple buddies and they would cruise around town. The other guys loved Stan's car, too. They dropped the "Brown" so now the car was just the "Bomber." They called it a "Babe-Catcher." Tory told them to shut up 'cause the Bomber might overhear their praises, get a big head and blow a gas-ket. Just then the Bomber backfired ... they looked at each other for a long questioning moment and then laughed out loud.

When Saturday morning arrived, Tory was visiting Stan, Isabel and Anne. After eating a second apple cinnamon turnover, the four friends climbed into the Bomber for a visit to the local farmers' market just to look around. It was a beautiful day to be out and about. It was warm enough for Tory to pull off his green and white Michigan State sweatshirt and tie it around his waist. He went to check out the natural honey table. He was interested in the process bees used to make that delicious golden nectar. The guy behind the outdoor counter wore bib-overalls and a red checkered shirt. He was small and had a high-pitched voice. He told Tory that bees start the honey process by visiting flowers and with their tongues they suck sweet nectar from the blossoms. He said that the bees have a special stomach just for the nectar and when that stomach is full, they fly back to the hive and store the nectar in honeycombs. The flapping of the bees' wings dries the nectar causing the beginning of a complex process that ends up in his jars as thick sweet honey. Tory was thinking about buying one of the jars except that honey was expensive. He was mentally counting the money he had in his wallet.

Anne was a few booths away looking at all the flowers in pots, Stan was sitting on a bench in the warm sun just enjoying the day and Isabel was, of course, checking out the bakery wares. She noticed a sign at the bakery booth that said "Free Samples". So, she helped herself to a frosted gingerbread boy cookie.

When Tory and Anne caught up with Isabel she was choking, spitting and gagging. Her eyes were watering, she coughed as she was trying to mop the cookie out her mouth with a tissue.

"What happened to you?" Anne asked as she put her arm around Isabel.

"All I did was try to eat a little free cookie from that bakery over there. It tasted terrible. I think I'm going to be sick," she moaned.

Tory looked over at the bakery. "Is that where you got the cookie?" he asked as he pointed to the booth where Isabel had indeed found the free sample.

"Yes," said Isabel as she gagged again.

Tory bent over laughing uncontrollably. "Look," he said. "Read the sign."

"So, yes I can read that sign," she said as she dabbed at her watering eyes. "It says K-9 Bakery."

"It is a CANINE BAKERY," he explained. "Isabel, you just ate some dog food." He roared with laughter exposing his even white teeth and deep dimples.

Isabel was not amused. *What would the Americans think of next … a bakery for dogs?*

Tory asked her if she was going to want to chase cars now, bury bones and turn around three times before she lies down. She did not see the humor in this although she couldn't stop a little giggle of her own because Tory was weak from laughing so hard at her. She tried to defend herself by telling him that the ladies behind the counter watched her put the cookie in her mouth and did nothing to stop her or at least warn her that their cookies were not for human consumption.

Tory said, "Well, maybe they just thought you had a little persnickety dog at home and were testing the goodies before you bought some for him."

He could hardly keep standing. He was doubled up laughing so hard that he had to join Stan on the bench. Stan patted him on the shoulder, although he wasn't quite sure why Tory had stumbled over to the bench and practically fell on him. Isabel offered Tory no assistance. She just strutted right by them, head held high and started towards to the parking lot to find the Bomber.

Later that same week when Anne was exactly nine months and three days along, her water broke. She called softly to Isabel while tapping on her door.

Isabel then woke Stan and grabbed up some towels and helped Anne out to the car. Stan called over to Tory's house and asked if Tory could drive them in the Bomber to the hospital.

Anne was riding shotgun while Tory drove. Isabel was in the backseat hanging over the front seat holding Anne's hand who was sitting on the towels because her water broke and she was leaking. Stan sat next to Isabel in the back quietly praying as he didn't know what else to do. Not one of the four knew anything about giving birth. It was nearly midnight when they arrived at the hospital. The attendants immediately took Anne to an observation room.

Anne said yes to the epidural. Soon an anesthetic, by way of a hypodermic needle, was introduced into the space around the spinal cord, relieving her of much of the pain. Her little boy was born at 2:30 A.M. He was perfect in every way. He weighed seven pounds six ounces and was twenty inches long with a little bit of fuzzy blonde hair. Isabel and Tory just stood and stared at the tiny-wrinkled baby. Stan had found a chair to sit in because of his wobbly legs. Tory was trying to imagine how that little guy could come out of Anne's body. What a mystery that was! He wasn't aware that the doctor had performed an episiotomy cutting Anne's vagina to make a larger passage for the baby to be pushed out into the doctor's waiting hands.

Isabel was holding the precious little bundle when she asked Anne if she had picked out a name for him.

"Not really," Anne said. "I didn't know if it would be a he or a she. What do you think would be a good name for him now that you see him?" Anne asked Isabel. Anne was teary eyed and exhausted. The epidural was beginning to wear off and now she was feeling a burning sensation between her legs.

Isabel didn't hesitate. She had been hoping to be asked. "What do you think about the name *Joseph*... after Stan's son, my late husband?" She looked hopefully at Anne.

Anne was weak. She was fighting to stay awake. She thought for a minute and said, "Yes... Yes, we'll name him Joseph. Joseph Stanley but we'll call him

Joey. Okay? Good, that's settled!" Her eyelids fluttered and she promptly fell into a well-deserved sleep.

Three days later Isabel and Tory went to the hospital to bring Anne and Joey home. Joey would share Anne's room where they had squeezed a crib and changing table into the back corner.

Stan needed a handkerchief to blow his nose and wipe his eyes when he heard the baby would be called Joseph Stanley... Joey for short. When Anne put her little baby in his arms, Stan was filled with such tenderness. Old memories of another little boy who was put in his arms years ago came back to his aging mind. He lowered his head and thanked God for this beautiful child. A tender love filled every corner of this little home.

Time seemed to be passing quickly. Little Joey was growing and getting stronger every day. All the while, Stan seemed to be shrinking as he was growing weaker. His heart was failing and his breathing was getting shallow. He was tired so much of the time and slept on and off all day in his easy chair listening to the radio. He was also spending hours in front of the TV watching his beloved Detroit Tigers or the Detroit Lions. At mealtime his appetite wasn't good anymore and he couldn't remember much of anything. He even stopped trying to cheat at cards. He repeated himself constantly, telling the same stories over and over. Stan was beginning to see shadows of people who weren't really there. Sometimes he asked Isabel about the people who were standing beside him... when in reality, no one else was in the room. Isabel always answered him the same way by saying, "I guess they're just some friends."

The fateful evening arrived when Stan couldn't seem to stay awake. He kept slumping over in his chair. His complexion was gray. The whites of his eyes were no longer white but were yellowish in color. Isabel and Anne were concerned and quietly sat with him. Joey was asleep in Anne's arms, when all of a sudden Stan spoke out loud in a weak, unsteady voice. He said, "Joe, Joe is that you?"

"What is it?" asked Anne. "Do you want to hold Joey?"

"No." whispered Stan. "Not Joey... It's *my* Joe."

With that, Stan looked towards the heavens and with tears streaming down his rugged old face, he lifted his arms for his son. He slumped back into his chair as his spirit left his earthly body. His face radiated peace. Their dear Stan was at rest.

Isabel and Anne had grown to truly love this special old man. They knew that they would miss him forever. He had saved them when each was hopeless with nowhere to turn and no one to turn to.

Arrangements were made for his burial. At a small informal memorial service, Tory was the only speaker. He spoke of Stan with such affection. *He said he knew on that terrible day when he had jumped to Stan's rescue, that Stan would have done the same for him. Stan would have given his life for me and I knew it. He said because of Stan, a family-like unit had evolved around him. Isabel and Anne were like big sisters to him. Little Joey was like a ray of sunshine on a rainy day. He said his love for Stan would be unending. There would be a place for Stan in his heart forever and his life would never be the same without him. It was as though a piece of a beautiful puzzle was missing and was never to be found again in this lifetime.*

A few days later, while thinking of Stan, Isabel opened the tin box that belonged to him. It held some personal papers including his last will and testament. Stan had left his house and money to Isabel. There was enough to send Anne to physical therapy school and enough to sustain Isabel for her lifetime, if she were careful. He left the Brown Bomber to Tory.

"Well, in that case," said Tory. "I've got some work to do."

He was planning a little facelift for that old car he loved. He cut two holes in the rear package tray (that's the ledge behind the rear seat). He installed two new speakers and covered the rest of that area with thick carpeting. Then he hooked up a power booster to the speakers. This was now a "bad boy" mobile. He dropped the 'er' on Bomber and his car was now known as the "Bomb."

On September 1, Tory got behind the wheel of the Bomb, looked up at the sky with long salute to his buddy Stan way up there somewhere and left for Ferris Institute in Big Rapids to enroll in the police academy. He tooted the Bomb's horn and waved at his favorite girls, Isabel and Anne, as he slowly drove by Stan's house, the house where he grew from a boy into a man. Tory threw a big kiss to Joey who was in Isabel's arms kicking his little feet and giggling. They were watching through the front window as Tory smiled his big handsome smile and drove off into his future.

The next morning, Anne gathered what she needed for school while Isabel tended to Joey. Each time Isabel heard Joey giggle, she tried to catch and hold the sound in her mind. When she closed her eyes at night, she always said goodnight to Joe and then to Stan imagining them together in heaven. After that, she would think of little Joey, his delightful sweetness and his happy little face. She would smile to herself just thinking of how Joey squirmed with delight when she tickled his chubby little toes. Isabel no longer had bad dreams of a baby crying out for her in the night . . . the elusive baby she could never find.

When Isabel had the miscarriage and lost Joe's baby, an emptiness had overwhelmed her. Her womb was empty and it seemed that her entire being was empty. That emptiness had taken more of her the day she was told that Joe would never be coming back to her. With her father's death more emptiness took her. Then when Isabel watched her mother die, the emptiness consumed her, leaving her with deep dark loneliness. Depression soon filled her emptiness and swallowed her.

That was then.

But now, Isabel was happy... really happy. It began when Stan reached out to her in love and filled some of that emptiness. Then Tory's enthusiastic friendship and dimpled smile filled some more of the emptiness. Anne, dear Anne, was like a sister to her, filling even more of that dark emptiness. And Joey? Well that little one provided the unconditional love that filled her to overflowing. There was no longer any room for depression or loneliness.

Isabel had transformed Stan's old bedroom into a cheery room for Joey. She painted the walls a soft shade of blue that matched the baby's eyes. In the corner was a toy chest made from Stan's old tool box. She knew that Stan would be happy to know that he gave his room to Joey who played in that back room for hours where there would always be a hint of Stan's presence remaining.

Anne was not in touch with her parents. She missed them. There were times she picked up the phone to call them and tell them about their delightful grandson. She always hung up the phone before they answered. Someday, when she was ready, she would wait for them to say, "Hello." If time really did heal all wounds, she would see them again. As for the young man who had gotten her pregnant, she completely lost track of him. She assumed he didn't know he was the father of a remarkable little boy. She worried about the day when Joey would be old enough to ask about his daddy. She just couldn't think about that right now.

Anne was excited to be starting a four-year program which was only a twenty-five-minute drive from Stan's. This house was truly her home now. She was a little nervous that today her physical therapy studies were really beginning.

As she was getting into her car, Isabel was standing out on the porch, smiling and holding Joey. Isabel gently took Joey's little arm and helped him wave bye-bye to his mommy. Anne's eyes were tearing up while Isabel and Joey threw kisses at her as she eased her car down the driveway and slowly drove off. The two of them watched Anne's car disappear into the cool, early morning mist.

Now alone, Joey was still cuddled in Isabel's arms. She turned her head to look down at him just as he looked up at her. As their eyes met... *their hearts started to cry.*